HUMANS'
ENHANCEMENTS

CLASHING REVELATIONS TRILOGY: BOOK 1

HUMANS' ENHANCEMENTS

I.M. STOICUS

Paperback ISBN: 978-1-63337-761-5
Hardback ISBN: 978-1-63337-762-2
E-book ISBN: 978-1-63337-763-9

HUMANS' ENHANCEMENTS is dedicated to the author's loving and wonderful family, as well as the memory of his deceased parents. May his devoted parents and father-in-law be in heaven with God and His glory. As wisely revealed in Revelations 21:4: *"God will wipe away every tear from their eyes; there shall be no more death, nor sorrow, nor crying. There shall be no more pain, for the former things have passed away."*

1.

DAY 1: THE AWAKENING

AN INNOCENT NEWBORN, who was clearly not an infant, was striving to be conscious from a deep slumber for the first time in his or her unknown existence.

The bewildered and confused newborn pondered, *Am I dreaming? What is a dream? I remember nothing; however, I possess a language with definitions. What is a language? Is this language my personal language that I have imagined and created in my mind with my own definitions? If that is true, I may understand no one else. Does a world exist outside of my mind? What is a world? Is there anyone or anything else? Am I utterly alone? I do not know!*

Equally important, am I real? Am I alive? Perhaps I am a computer that has developed to possess a consciousness. What is a computer? What is consciousness? I do not remember what I am because I have experienced nothing. I have never felt pain or love? What is pain? What is love? I am experiencing with no realization of what I am. Am I only able to contemplate? This could just be a nightmare. What is a nightmare? I have all these words and concepts with no experience in relating to them. Obviously, my unrecognizable existence is nascent. Logically, I must exist since I am experiencing something, but I do not know how I exist. However, I ironically understand and know the definitions, which makes me feel extremely bizarre. I feel completely confused.

Unfortunately, I may be just a sophisticated conscious computer that has just been activated. Maybe, I will soon be inactivated. I have sensed nothing from any of my senses that I would possess if I were alive. However, what does it mean to be alive? I do not remember using any of my senses. What are senses?

Wait! I think I see a light, a glaring bright white light! I believe that I hear or perceive something, or someone. I do not understand what the sounds mean. Wait, I sense something! I hear the sounds of words! What are words?

A voice commanded loudly, "Awaken and be! Visualize and perceive for the first time!"

For the first moment, the newborn realized that she or he could see and hear. She or he realized that she or he possessed senses that indicated he or she might be human or an animal.

The newborn pondered to himself or herself, ***Whose voice is this? I do not know. It sounds automated. He or she, I guess, has no emotional expressions on his or her face. I feel awkward, since I have these skills and abilities without knowing how I acquired these abilities. I probably acquired them instinctively. I believe that I am correctly identifying this about this new, unfamiliar presence. However, all my thoughts, feelings, and experiences are happening for the first time. I may be wrong. I do not know! I feel amazed and overwhelmed with this experience.***

The newborn became concerned with the current situation because he or she had no experience from which to recall. Moreover, he or she struggled to speak for the first time. He or she fought to verbalize.

"Who, who am I? What, what am I? And where, where am I?" asked the newborn who was striving to gain his or her consciousness and understanding.

The unknown, expressionless, stoic individual responded with confidence. "You are waking up for the first time as a designated male at birth. Your all-knowing STATE-approved given identification number and current STATE-awarded name is **XY777-316**. I shall henceforth refer to you as **316** for abbreviation. You are in a benevolent STATE Development Center."

The newborn continued to daydream. *Am I just an identification number? I do not have a name. That is depressing. What is this supposed all-knowing STATE? The unknown individual told me that I am in a STATE Development Center, which means very little to me. Furthermore, I believe that he or she is a robot. However, I may be a robot or human. I do not know.*

The unknown, heartless individual continued to speak. "If I may take the liberty, this facility is one of the finest STATE Development Centers. It is scheduled for modernization because the facility is deficient in some STATE required upgrades. Some upgrades needed are monitoring devices in operating rooms and in enhancers' offices.

"For your information, **316**, you are just rousing from your developmental coma, which is 1,666 days, including conception. You have the maturity level and physicality of an eighteen-year-old biological male human."

All AE HUMANS were artificially inseminated with genetically modified and enhanced egg and sperm. The AE HUMAN developmental process had been accelerated to practically over four times the normal human developmental period. All AE

HUMANS were artificially developed in a non-natural womb initially; then, an enhancer transferred the AE HUMAN to a controlled artificial incubator, which was AI controlled. The STATE did not allow any unauthorized births. The STATE oversaw the entire process to ensure defects were eliminated. If an AE HUMAN fell below standards, it was immediately terminated. All experiences during this period were overridden by the initial chip, which was installed a couple weeks before initial awakening.

316 thought to himself, *I have been in a coma for 1,666 days, and now I possess the maturity and physicality of an eighteen-year-old. This makes no sense to me. Have I just been activated?*

"That is fascinating. Who or what are you? What is a biological human?" 316 had a plethora of questions and thoughts that were coming to his mind.

"First, I am your STATE-assigned overseer. Second, I am an Artificial Intelligent Robot, model number AI thirteen, male version. Refer to me as AI Thirteen. Third, a biological human is a living, rational animal. Well, they have a tendency to be irrational. Finally, to avoid an overabundance of repetitive questions, you must close your eyes and ask yourself to define and image whatever you wish to understand. So, to test this function, ask yourself to define and image the word 'human.' Tell me the definition and image you recall?" said AI Thirteen.

316 thought to himself, *AI Thirteen is a robot, and I believe that he is probably my devoted assigned instructor.* 316 responded with certainty, "The definition of a 'human' is a rational animal that developed from primates. Their sex is male or

female and may be, at occasions, genderless. Humans can reproduce like other animals. Humans historically had parents and families. All humans are inferior to ELITES and CZARS. I see a detailed image of both a male and female human."

AI Thirteen replied with approval. "That is superb! Your language chip is functioning properly. I still want to determine if your other software is functioning properly, which must be to STATE-approved standards."

"Do you know who my parents are?" asked **316** emotionally.

"You do not have any assigned parents, nor do you possess a mother or a father. The beloved and all-knowing, benevolent STATE has deemed that parents, mothers, and fathers are no longer necessary. The ancient practice of parenting by biological humans has been deemed inefficient and undesirable for the GREAT STATE. Obviously, the all-knowing and loving STATE has assigned me to monitor your progress. I shall preserve your proper development. I am here to safeguard that the WILL and the DETERMINATION of the GREAT STATE are achieved by approved standards. Furthermore, to avoid any other relationship questions, adhere to this. The all-knowing STATE has deemed families as unnecessary for the greater good. Equally important, you, as an AE HUMAN, do not need to be raised by a family, especially parents, as stated. The AE HUMAN'S developmental period, from conception to adulthood, has been substantially improved over biological humans. It is significantly faster and more efficient. You should be a fully functional adult by day six. Biological humans took well over eighteen years to develop into adulthood. Thus, the GREAT STATE has determined your physical attributes in order to establish that you reach adulthood in six days. Their requirements equalized STATE outcomes that must be obeyed and accomplished," declared AI Thirteen.

"Oh, what am I transforming into or becoming? Am I a robot or not?" asked **316** inquisitively.

"You are developing into an AE HUMAN with the all-knowing STATE-approved uploads after being in an artificial womb and incubator. 'AE' is an acronym for 'Artificially Enhanced.' Thus, you are becoming an Artificially Enhanced Human. You possess an initial chip. The chip requires upgrades via your installed porthole equipped with synthetic memory system with advance upload capabilities.

"You are benefiting from the STATE-approved language upload within the chip, as well as other STATE-approved knowledge uploads. The greatness of the STATE has ameliorated AE HUMAN property with upgraded enhancements that pure biological humans would never have achieved via natural evolution. This results in superior AE HUMANS that will serve unquestionably and adore the GREAT STATE. As you are discovering, you are able to speak and read the current approved STATE language," informed AI Thirteen.

"So, you will love and care for me?" **316** said emotionally.

"Of course not! I am not here to love you or to show any feelings or emotions toward you. Obviously, I am here to protect and safeguard that the desired WILL of the all-knowing STATE is achieved. This includes your allegiance and commitment to the GREAT STATE. I do not possess any feelings like a biological human or an AE HUMAN. My programming secures total and complete allegiance to the all-knowing GREAT STATE.

"The GREAT STATE has determined that an AE HUMAN has six days to ask questions without adverse consequences. However, my response is not required and I may choose to be silent. This is DAY ONE of your initial awakening as well as your initial day at age zero. Therefore, do you, **316**, have any additional questions?" declared AI Thirteen.

Oh, AI Thirteen is a cold, heartless robot. He is here to monitor and oversee me. I have no parents, family, or loved ones. I wonder why I crave love. I guess that it is instinctive. The GREAT STATE is concerning to me. My existence seems to be an existence only for the GREAT STATE. However, I do not know how to feel, 316 concluded to himself.

"You mentioned previously that the STATE has required outcomes. What do you mean by outcomes? I assume they are not required to be equal completely?" asked the inquisitive **316**.

AI Thirteen's face flushed an alarming red color. "You are fortunate that you are still within your six-day grace period. No, all AE HUMANS are identified by six STATE safeguarded group identities. Furthermore, the STATE meticulously monitors these six STATE safeguarded group identities. This is to make certain that the outcomes are what the GREAT STATE has deemed them to be. The six STATE-approved and safeguarded group identities are:

Genders,
Class,
Origins,
Religions,
Colors,
and Age Groups.

"Since all AE HUMANS are deemed by the all-knowing STATE as manufactured equal to each other, outcomes MUST be equal.. There are no exceptions. You are created by the STATE for the STATE. You have no divine purpose. Your self-interest is meaningless to the STATE. The ONLY accepted interest is the STATE'S interest. The STATE'S interest controls the AE HUMAN'S attributes that will exist, as well as which ones that have been deemed never to be again. In addition, all AE HUMANS are STATE property. All STATE property must adhere to the standards and laws of the STATE. However, since the ALL-KNOWING STATE cares for its property, all AE HUMANS' needs are taken care of by the STATE. Of course, all your STATE-determined needs are fulfilled. You occupy and possess nothing, and the GREAT STATE will confirm your happiness as well as determine your purpose. Therefore, all of your needs will be matched to the determined STATE-willed outcome.

"The GREAT STATE has eliminated many unnecessary human experiences and phases of life, like old age and childhood. The GREAT STATE ensures that the human population's numbers are manageable and minimal. This is to prevent humans from becoming parasitic and harmful toward the planet, Gaia," proclaimed AI Thirteen.

The STATE is all-powerful and insists that it is all-knowing. I guess I should be happy since the STATE ensures it; however, I doubt it. At what population number does the GREAT STATE think humans become parasitic? 316 reflected.

"Undoubtedly, I appreciate the reminder that I only have six days to ask STATE-unapproved questions. Please instruct and inform me about the six identity groups in order to serve the

STATE properly and legally," asked **316** with undetected cynicism.

"I shall educate you. I will begin with the identity group called age, which has six six-year cycles. Each cycle, of course, is only six years. You are in the first cycle. Once someone has finished their sixth cycle, then the all-knowing and compassionate STATE will recognize your dedication to the STATE. Next, the state will mercifully terminate you from your initial awakening at age thirty-six. As mentioned previously, and to avoid confusion, the STATE declares that today is your initial day; you are zero years old today," AI Thirteen stated.

Well, if the STATE is benevolent and compassionate, why would it kill its people and claim to be merciful? Is our existence that dreadful and tormented that we welcome our death? That is clearly a contradiction. I believe the GREAT STATE concluded that AE HUMANS are a burden after thirty-six years of age, **316** thought to himself.

"Why would the all-loving STATE terminate someone at thirty-six?" mocked **316**.

"Listen and obey, I am warning you! I can detect emotions, and I detect you are mocking the ALL-KNOWING STATE! However, I shall answer your inquiry. AE HUMANS still possess a biological human body. Obviously, the flawed and inferior AE-HUMAN body degenerates and gradually loses its ability to serve the GREAT STATE. The AE HUMAN body eventually becomes a burden to the GREAT STATE. This is unlike the superiority of an AI robot anatomical body like I possess," AI Thirteen arrogantly mocked.

Obviously, AI Thirteen believes he is superior to humans, **316** concluded to himself.

"So, all AE HUMANS exist for only thirty-six years?" **316** questioned as he doubted.

"No, there are five STATE-classified possibilities for existing less than thirty-six years:

"**First, AE HUMANS may experience accidental deaths while working for and serving the GREAT STATE. This possibility of death is clearly over twenty percent of all deaths prior to reaching thirty-six years.**

"**Second, they expire from natural or accidental causes such as tornadoes or diseases; however, diseases are reduced since the lion's share of AE HUMANS must be vaccinated monthly.**

"**Third, they are gloriously killed in war and should always be remembered for their celebrated service to the GREAT STATE. This classified possibility is clearly over forty percent of all deaths prior to reaching thirty-six years.**

"**Fourth, because of injuries or diseases or if they have become a burden to the STATE, they are mercifully ended by the STATE.**

"**Fifth, an AE HUMAN commits a STATE capital offense. This is thirty percent of the premature deaths,**" informed AI Thirteen.

"So, no one lives over thirty-six years?" asked **316**.

"This is best answered after informing you about the five classifications and the additional protected groups:

"**The first classification, soldiers, is required to be in military service for a minimum of four years. If they are successful and survive, they may advance to the second or fourth classification. Soldiers are not vaccinated monthly. They are awarded and fed very well when successful.**

"The second classification is the laborers and technicians. They serve the STATE as farmers to machine operators or equipment repairers. They may not advance to a higher class; however, they could request and be accepted as soldiers.

"The third classification is the professional category from enhancers to engineers to military officers. Military officers with four successful and distinguished years of combat and military service may advance to the fourth classification. In addition, other professionals may be deemed worthy by the GREAT STATE to advance to the fourth classification. Military officers, and others higher are not vaccinated monthly.

"The fourth classification is the honorable guardians and vanguards. The guardians have corresponding professional or military officer status. Furthermore, the honorable guardians are the professional advisors. In addition, the vanguards are the political enforcers and advisors for the STATE.

"The fifth classification is the ELITES and CZARS, which are the ELITE AE HUMANS who oversee and rule the GREAT STATE.

"This is a significant amount of information, and I still have not answered your question. To ensure clarity, do you understand what I am saying so far?" emphasized AI Thirteen.

The GREAT STATE has created a hierarchy with the ELITES on top and soldiers at the bottom and others in between, 316 concluded to himself. "Yes, what classification am I becoming?" he asked.

"You are currently assigned to be developed as a first classification, a soldier. However, if you pass several requirements and tests, then you shall be given another three days. These three days will be used to be reclassified as a military officer with a specialty.

"Now, I shall discuss the five classifications regarding color and age limits. Remember that age, classification, and color are three of the six STATE-protected group identities. Thankfully, the GREAT and all-knowing STATE has declared that the five classifications shall each be assigned a color and an age limit:

"The first classification is made up of soldiers, and they wear red or green and have a maximum age of thirty-six years. Of course, the red is their dress uniform and the green battle dress is for combat or missions.

"The second classification is made up of the laborers and technicians, and they both wear white and also have the maximum age of thirty-six years.

"The third classification is comprised of the professionals and military officers, and they wear blue and also have a maximum age of thirty-six years. Officers wear green battle dress during combat and missions.

"The fourth classification is the guardians and vanguards, and they wear gold. Guardians and vanguards have the maximum age of sixty-six years and six days. During a guardian or vanguard's last six days, the all-knowing STATE determines if the guardian or vanguard advances to be an ELITE AE HUMAN or ended with STATE glory.

"The fifth classification is the ELITE AE HUMANS, and they wear black. They have no expiration date.

"Remember, no AE HUMAN may wear a color of a different classification. Second, they must wear the color of their classification. Wearing black is a capital offense for an AE

HUMAN. A last piece of information: The GREAT STATE only allows 0.666 percent of the population as either fourth or fifth classification. Do you comprehend what I have said?" asked AI Thirteen.

Well, I am at the bottom of the hierarchy. I am becoming a soldier; however, I could become an officer. I do not know if this goal is worthy or even obtainable. In addition, this existence is, without a doubt, a struggle with a significant amount of suffering, **316** thought to himself.

"Yes, please tell me about the STATE-approved genders," inquired **316**.

"The following are the three STATE-authorized genders:

Agender;

Male gender; and

Female gender.

"You are assigned to be a **male gender,** which is revealed in your identification number. The 'XY' indicates **male gender**. In addition, a **female gender** is 'XX,' and the **agender** is 'XXXY.' Tomorrow, during your physical AE HUMAN transformation, you will be transformed into an adult male gender. All other historically debated genders have been removed from consideration by the GREAT STATE. There are ONLY three allowed genders. It is a capital offense to recognize any other gender or failure to properly recognize someone of their assigned gender; however, the STATE is merciful since the offended individual MUST allow one warning and express their STATE-assigned gender. Clearly, the STATE never errs in determining that your sex and gender are in harmony and synchronization. The STATE safeguards that there is a correct match for all AE

HUMANS. Moreover, the GREAT STATE terminates any unapproved mutations. The GREAT STATE does not err; THE STATE is perfect!

"In addition, all forms of sexual relations among AE HUMANS are capital offenses. Of course, there is an exception for sexual relationship with an ELITE AE HUMAN. The all-knowing STATE never miscalculates and will always protect that your body matches your sexual orientation. Since you will not be a pure biological human, this will be achieved. The GREAT STATE protects that you will not be burdened with any sexual desires or gender confusion," counseled AI Thirteen.

"Well, how will I be physically different?" asked **316**.

"To begin with, I will tell you how you will be similar to everyone else:

"First, all male gender and agender AE HUMANS are six feet tall. Female gender AE HUMANS are five feet and six inches tall. However, ELITES and vanguards are six feet and six inches tall. This emphasizes that all AE HUMANS must look up to an ELITE and vanguards.

"All AE HUMANS have dark black hair and brown eyes; however, ELITES have wisdom white hair and crimson eyes. Your skin color will be brown, which is true for all classes except the ELITE. The ELITE skin color is pure genuine white.

"Most other body parts will be similar to a biological human, such as two arms and two legs. Since you are an AE HUMAN, you will have an upload porthole at the back of your neck. In addition, since you shall be a soldier, you will be physically enhanced to be a better fighter with exceptional endurance. Do you grasp what I have stated so far?" asked AI Thirteen.

Well, I will be a six-foot-tall male with black hair and brown eyes. I see that I already have brown skin. Oh, if that is a mirror and I am seeing my reflection, then my hair and eyes are already the STATE-approved colors. This is fantastic! That is one less concern! **316** thought to himself, delighted.

"Yes, but I believe you still need to discuss two more safeguarded group identities: religion and origin," stated **316**.

"That is an affirmative! You have been attentive and focused. I shall next discuss the protected group identity religion. There are no allowed religion groups except the GREAT STATE and the ELITES.

"No AE HUMANS may practice or adhere to a religion. Furthermore, no AE HUMAN may proselytize any religions that are not STATE approved. No AE HUMAN nor any religion is above the ALL-KNOWING AND JUST STATE. It is, of course, a capital offense to place any religion above the GREAT STATE except for the ELITES. There is no god or religion above the STATE. In addition, both the ELITES and vanguards, who have been revealed to be loyal disciples of the GREAT STATE, wear a *silver necklace.* This necklace has either a letter 'A' or 'S' around their neck to indicate their religious devotion. Do you understand so far?" asked AI Thirteen.

316 determined to himself, *There is only one religion, the GREAT STATE; however, there is an exception for the ELITE, which is a noticeably common theme. Why would you have the death penalty for believing in God or gods? Of course, everyone must know the classification structure. I wonder what the "A" and "S" stand for?* "Yes, please explain origins," requested **316**.

"Finally, I shall next discuss the protected group identity origin. There are eight origin groups, which are also the eight empires of the world:

Brazilian Empire;
Russian Soviet Empire;
Raising Son Maoist Empire;
Germanic Nazi Empire;
Indian Empire;
Marxist Mao Empire;
Aztec Empire; and,
Federal Republic Empire.

"Our origin and loyalty are to the **Federal Republic EMPIRE.** All eight empires strive to coexist. All eight empires belong and adhere to the **Globalist Legislative Unified Enterprise or GLUE.** The GLUE is the world's ruling body, which is incorporated globally. Be aware that we, the Federal Republic Empire, have been at war with the Aztec Empire for generations.

"All origins MUST respect one another, and the warring empires guarantee that their enemy dies with honor and glory. Presently, all eight empires are at war with one other empire. In addition, GLUE has required that the world population not exceed four billion AE HUMANS. This is half of what the world's population was antebellum to the GREAT WAR. Each empire is expected not to exceed five-hundred million AE HUMANS. There are eight-thousand vanguards in the world. Each empire is allowed six ELITES. There are **eighteen GLUE Ruling ELITES**. Thus, there are sixty-six ELITES in the world. There are eighteen ELITES that are the GLUE Ruling ELITES and are gloriously called czars. The czars are omnipotent and no other ELITE will challenge them. Czars wear the same color outfit and necklace as an ELITE. Czars also wear a silver crown with the same corresponding letter 'A' or 'S' as their necklace. You will learn more about the czars later. I think that this is enough for your first day.

"I shall now lead you to your recovery room in order for you to rest, since tomorrow will be a significant drain on your imperfect human body," AI Thirteen said with obvious mockery.

That is great! I cannot wait to hear about the czars that are feared by all. Obviously, the GLUE will bring us all together like actual glue, 316 mocked to himself.

AI Thirteen led him to the recovery room and pointed toward the bed. AI Thirteen commanded, "Lay on the bunk and go to sleep!"

316 tried to close his eyes and rest. AI Thirteen sat on a chair and monitored him.

316 was quiet and pensive. As he was resting, he contemplated, *Who or what am I? I have been assigned an identification number by the alleged GREAT STATE, 316. I possess a language; however, I do not know how. AI Thirteen stated that I have an initial chip. This seems to be additional evidence that I am just a sophisticated computer or artificial being. However, AI Thirteen, who does not care for me, stated I am a biological human, but I will be artificially enhanced. Whatever does that mean?*

I learned that all AE HUMANS are identified by six STATE-protected group identities with five classifications. Of course, the ELITE is at the top of the food chain. There is a clear hierarchal structure with five classifications, with the ELITES on the top and the soldiers on the bottom.

I feel utterly alone and confused. This is, without a doubt, not a sympathetic existence; but is a detached existence with suffering and misery. Of course, I still have not experienced suffering. So far, I have only experienced concepts and words, as well as a plethora of rules and draconian laws.

I do not know how to feel about becoming a soldier that will fight for the Federal Republic Empire. In addition, the war has been occurring for generations with the same rival, the Aztec Empire.

I only have five days left to ask unapproved questions. Of course, AI Thirteen may refuse to answer many of my questions.

316 felt fatigued from his first exhausting day. He fell into a deep sleep. AI Thirteen continued to monitor him.

DAY 2: THE TRANSFORMATION

IT WAS JUST AFTER DAWN when AI Thirteen arrived at **316's** chambers. **316** was barely awake when the robot forced him out of bed and onto the toilet, where he was commanded to imbibe his mandatory medication. AI Thirteen instructed **316** to completely excrete his stool, and then wait at least five additional minutes to avoid any accidents.

"Next, you must take a shower in the automatic wash next to the commode. To assist you in understanding these commands, remember to close your eyes and ask yourself to define and image what you need to know and comprehend," AI Thirteen directed.

316 thought to himself, *What does excrete your stool mean? According to my downloads, I must sit on this commode and wait. This is extremely awkward.* **316** excreted his stool, which was extremely painful. This was agonizing because he was excreting the highly technologically advanced chemicals and nano devices that accelerated his development. The commode flushed at least three times automatically during the laborious ordeal. He was in extreme agony. He waited over five minutes, then he experienced his first shower. The automatic wash was very efficient, and he felt spotless and refreshed for the first time in his life. As **316** left the lavatory, AI Thirteen handed him a red robe. **316** robed himself with the needed assistance of AI Thirteen.

AI Thirteen commanded, "Follow me!" AI Thirteen directed him to another room down the hall where there was a middle-aged enhancer wearing gold clothing. The gold clearly meant that he was also a guardian.

"An enhancer is a qualified and educated professional that enhances and transforms a biological human into an AE HUMAN via artificial and medical methods," AI Thirteen explained.

This enhancer specialized in enhancing soldiers, first classification, and officers, third or fourth classifications. The office was well lit, and the room was pure white with an advanced medical bed and futuristic medical equipment. Equally important, the medical quarters were extremely clean and organized.

The enhancer insisted, "**316**, please remove your robe and lay on the medically enhanced bed." **316** closed his eyes to understand the commands, then he obeyed. Next, the enhancer injected something in **316**'s arm, and he immediately fell asleep. The enhancer then walked behind AI Thirteen, and he inactivated him.

The enhancer pondered to himself, *Before I leave this empty and tormented life, I shall perform something right for humanity. So help me, God.*

Honestly, I realize that I am part of the problem and I must be part of the solution. I recognize that I am responsible for my actions, as well as my lack of actions. I definitely have not been conscientious enough. Furthermore, I have been a disgraced coward, and I have been merely an appeaser. I must strive always to be responsible for my decisions and speak the truth. Moreover, I must set the example of a good person. I must adhere to the lesson of Mathew 23:12: "And whosoever shall exalt himself shall be abased; and he that shall humble himself shall be exalted."

This is what the ELITES and others cannot comprehend or care to understand: Once individuals and government build a society on lies and malevolent behavior, even for the purpose or ultimate end toward a desired utopia, that society will become an inferno and wicked. Enhancer Aristides and his assistant had discussed many times how their actions were part of the problem. They felt a great guilt over how the nation and people had become. They realized that history was replete with false promises of utopias that always required the surrender of rights to the state in return for so-called security.

The enhancer was interrupted by someone entering the room who resembled an AI robot in height and stature. The enhancer stated with delight, "Good morning, Aphrodite! We have a busy and purposeful day." Aphrodite turned on the security system that blocked the ability of the STATE to monitor their actions and conversations.

The enhancer smiled and felt blessed to have Aphrodite. He thought that she had a witty sense of humor and possessed some extremely beautiful feminine qualities. Furthermore, her smile enhanced her lovely black hair and gorgeous brown eyes. Of course, she possessed an extremely attractive, womanly physique. Her youthful presence and her personality illuminated any room and always brightened his day. He also thought that she was an exceptional medical specialist who worked with kindness and devotion. He blushed, and he shook the feelings away; however, she knew his true feelings.

The enhancer diligently operated on **316.** He had a sophisticated holograph to assist him, which was an additional helper besides Aphrodite. This holograph was another of Aristides' creations, made to improve his craft.

Specialist Aphrodite removed AI Thirteen to an adjacent room, then returned to assist the enhancer. The enhancer installed a life support and monitoring device into **316**. After the awakening, these required STATE procedures determined if the subject could continue to exist; the STATE was always striving to avoid using limited STATE resources and prevent expenditure. All AE HUMANS must have their benefits exceed their costs.

The enhancer said joyfully, "Aphrodite, do you know what we are undertaking today and who this is?"

Aphrodite smiled delightfully. "Yes, I know! We shall do what is right, according to Almighty God. Of course, we, as always, shall be contrary to the tyrannical and evil STATE. I always love committing treason with you! In addition, we are enhancing the beloved chosen one!

"By the way, I shall first examine the chosen one's genetic DNA code while you are creating the upgraded porthole in his neck and removing his initial chip. Next, we shall ensure that **316** receives all the upgrades as if he is a military officer and guardian or vanguard. I believe your desire is that he should be a 'Q' combat engineer. And, of course, we will implement model 17 upgrades, which provide for freewill and critical reasoning."

"Aphrodite, you know me too well. You are the only specialist that I trust," the enhancer expressed with delight and a loving smile.

She wondered pleasantly to herself, *I am so ecstatic that enhancer Aristides is in my life. I thank the good Lord for bringing him to me and that he loves God as much as I do.*

He is my knight in shining armor because he has saved me from a life of torment and poverty. Thank God that he is an exceptional and compassionate enhancer. His compassion and love resulted in saving my life after I was seriously injured in the war and lost my right arm. My artificial arm has an identification chip in it that says that I am an AI robot, which allows me to avoid detection of being an AE woman and from the Aztec Empire.

Aristides may be significantly older than I am. I believe that he is in his forties because he is a guardian and must have passed the thirty-six-year-old AE HUMAN limit. He has some gray hair, which gives him that handsome look of wisdom. Of course, his wisdom is just and fair to all. Furthermore, I am so fortunate that he is extremely intelligent; he has created numerous items that assist us in preventing being detected. I truly love him.

She smiled. "Yes, I know. You know that we shall take longer to complete the wanted enhancements and transformation than is allotted for **316** by the tyrannical STATE. I recommend that I be blamed because I needed a recharge for three hours. I will send a message up four hours prior to our deadline."

"Aphrodite, you are correct; please tell me their response. I want nothing to happen to you. By the way, please reprogram AI Thirteen," the enhancer expressed reluctantly.

"I shall keep you informed. The good news is that there is no requirement for a gender transformation for **316**. He is already a fully functional and anatomically developed male. The test results came back, and he has no STATE-unapproved DNA deformities. He has progressed well for the last 1,667 days.

"We primarily want to ensure that the upgraded porthole is inserted properly in the back of his neck. Since **316** was artificially conceived, we ought to safeguard that he has the ability to avoid transmitted commands from the tyrannical STATE;

however, he must know the commands," Aphrodite said with a wink and a smile.

Aphrodite worked meticulously on AI Thirteen as she teased, "By the way, you are a wise and knowledgeable guardian and enhancer. In addition, I would add, an excellent deceiver and traitor to the tyrannical STATE. My dear love, what will be his name? I am sick and tired of calling him by a heartless, cold assigned number."

"His God-given name will be Solon. His name has been approved by the GREAT STATE. However, his identification number will be similar, **XY777-316-Q17-0001**," the enhancer responded with delight.

Aphrodite smiled with joy and stated, "Aristides, you have given him an excellent name. Solon was an Athenian sage and a philosopher. He will bestow wisdom to the desperate, depressed, and impoverished human race."

"Aphrodite, God willing, humanity will become wiser. We are attempting to slay Goliath with merely a sling and a stone. The evil Goliath is the all-mighty STATE. In addition, we pray others are willing and preparing to take on the totalitarian STATE. We hope that there are plenty of other natural born humans. I believe that there are humans like Solon, since the endless wars are merely a cover-up and deception to hunt them down. In addition, these endless wars are to maintain the world population supposedly at four billion, which is grossly inaccurate. The oppressive STATE yearns and craves to purge all natural unenhanced humans from the planet. Their goal is to develop humans into another supposed new, superior, technically enhanced specie," Aristides replied.

"AI Thirteen has been reprogramed with your prime objective," Aphrodite happily responded.

"This is great! He is now programmed to obey Solon and to protect him at all costs, even when it conflicts with the EVIL STATE," Aristides responded.

Aphrodite joked, "Yes, AI Thirteen is also programmed to plant and love flowers. Aristides, you know I love flowers!"

Aristides said reassuringly, "Love, I got you a gorgeous pink lily and a pink orchard, which are in our domicile."

"Dear, I know. I saw the lovely flowers already. They are truly beautiful and they are one of God's greatest creations!" she stated in delight.

They saw the warning light at the door. She glanced at Aristides and he immediately nodded affirmatively toward her. Furthermore, she went to answer the door. She was challenged by a STATE investigator who was wearing gold clothing like Aristides.

The investigator inquired, "The STATE cannot monitor your progress, since this room has not been upgraded yet. We are aware that your area will be upgraded next month, and we have overcrowding in the facility. In addition, the STATE trusts your actions since your record is unblemished and you were awarded by ELITE Heraclitus. Is everything all right?"

Since the STATE had become overwhelmingly bureaucratic in order to subjugate their people, no one was willing to express when something was wrong or needed to be repaired. Complaining or expressing problems or needed corrections generally resulted in governmental officials wanting to cover up their incompetencies. The people learned to express what the STATE wanted to hear in order to avoid being punished, tortured, or eliminated. Remember, the STATE was perfect and never erred. Thus, truth was the first casualty, as everyone spoke lies to survive.

Aphrodite responded like a cold AI robot. "Yes, the transformation and enhancements are going as planned. There may be a delay since I shall need to be recharged. AI Thirteen, as you notice, is currently recharging, and I shall do so in approximately sixty-eight minutes from now."

The investigator replied, "Enhancer, if you desire, I could obtain another AI specialist to assist you while this AI specialist recharges."

Enhancer responded, "Thank you for the offer. Fortunately, I can perform my duties without an AI specialist. I shall serve the GREAT STATE. Furthermore, I will work overtime alone to safeguard that these enhancements and transformation are complete. I shall ensure that the mission is a success in glory to the GREAT STATE. I have performed these procedures previously without the assistance of an AI specialist. As you are aware, AI specialists are in short supply because of the glorious war."

The investigator said, "Yes! This is **IN SERVICE TO THE GREAT STATE!** Enhancer and guardian, carry on! I shall inform the higher that you shall work an extra four to six hours today. Your service is deeply appreciated! And I am aware of your exceptional record, as well as performing your duties without the help of an AI specialist. You are correct that STATE resources are limited because of the glorious WAR. As noted, this will look excellent on your record!"

"Thank you! I shall continue working now. Please have a laborer bring nutritional substances to me in two hours," the enhancer replied.

Investigator smiled and replied, "Of course, I shall do that! The nutritional substances will arrive in two hours. Carry on!" The STATE investigator left.

Aphrodite immediately secured the room. She was puzzled and confused. "Why did you ask him to do that?"

"The investigator must return anyway to finish his report. Now, I have a good idea when he will return with food, of course. In addition, he has an excuse to obtain extra food for himself and me without getting into trouble. Remember, we are doing this **IN SERVICE TO THE GREAT STATE**," Aristides replied confidently.

Aphrodite laughed and smiled. "That is why I love you. Of course, I love flowers as well!"

Aristides grinned. "I feel the same. Of course, I prefer you always, my *sine qua non*. However, I wish that we could have a romantic dinner that entailed a sirloin steak with a loaded potato."

She laughed. "You know that all the forbidden food is now contraband. All the alleged nutritional substances are synthetic. Of course, since you are a guardian, you are allowed bona fide food fourteen times a week."

He responded, "Yes, you are right.

"Oh! By the way, for full disclosure and truthfulness, I know why the investigator truly came. He is a successful military officer that was awarded the title of guardian because of his military accomplishments. I have treated him frequently before. He confided in me that he has terrible nightmares from his military campaigns. He did not discuss his true motivations since you were in the room and, obviously, no one trusts anyone anymore, which is terribly depressing."

"Well, we trust each other. Thank God! I will prepare the investigator's needed medication, and I shall place it on the table. Of course, you will prescribe him the non-approved medication PREVENTION PLUS. You, as an enhancer, can prescribe for experimentally approved reasons. We have shown numerous times that it is effective. However, as always, the GREAT bureaucratic STATE has their head up their you-know-what. They are idiots! When he comes, I will pretend to be charging in the adjacent room with AI Thirteen," she stated.

Aristides responded, "Thank you, dear! In a few minutes, I will need you to prevent Solon from slipping into a coma or possibly dying. I require you to assist me with his porthole. The computer-aided holograph and medically enhanced bed are not enough support. Obviously, I do not want to take any unnecessary risks. I have removed the initial chip that was attached to his spine."

Aphrodite said with sincere reassurance, "Aristides, God will protect your son. I shall be there in a minute. You are an excellent enhancer and a good man. Solon will fulfill his divine purpose." Aphrodite came to assist Aristides. They worked diligently, and they were successful with the upgraded installation.

Aristides spoke. "His upgraded porthole is technically superior to the ones installed for ELITE AE HUMANS. This installation will prevent the STATE from reading Solon's conscious thoughts and controlling him. His free will shall be maintained. Ironically, the STATE never acknowledges that it can read AE HUMANS' thoughts. Unfortunately, the STATE has removed most AE HUMANS' free will; they are merely biological computers. In addition, the destruction device will not be installed in Solon; however, Solon will be informed when the STATE pursues his termination. Solon will know his enemies' next moves, but the ELITE will not know his thoughts or his next move. They will not even have his vitals, except rudimentary ones. He will be a divine sovereign individual with a free will like you, my love."

The light signaled at the door. It had been nearly two hours since the investigator left. Aphrodite quickly placed the PREVENTION PLUS on the table. She went into the other room to pretend that she was charging.

The enhancer opened the door and stated, "Welcome! Please enter, Investigator Hephaestus. Be aware that both AI robots are charging. By the way, how are your nightmares?"

Investigator Hephaestus said, "My medicine ran out several days ago and the nightmares are severe. I wake up screaming in agony from reliving the battle in which I lost over eighty percent of my soldiers; however, we were victorious and terminated all the enemy soldiers, including civilians. Over one hundred thousand people died that victorious day for the glory of the STATE. The next day—and I regret not being there since I was in the rear for my injuries—the enemy regained the territory.

"I was fortunate that the STATE was willing to repair and heal me. I now have three artificial limbs and one artificial eye, as well as an artificial kidney. Unfortunately, my comrade of nearly four years died that glorious day with honor and glory, as well as the rest of my glorious brave division."

The investigator's face went completely blank. Moreover, he seemed to stare at something in the far distance.

The investigator reflected to himself, *I loathe this tyrannical evil STATE. The ELITES only care for themselves, and they are wicked. They are either satanic worshipers or atheists.*

The good news is that their house is divided. I do not trust any of them.

I fought in several battles that only resulted in death and misery. I lost my best friend and saw thousands and thousands of people die senselessly for the same meaningless piece of land.

I desire to trust the enhancer, but if I am wrong, then I would be executed for treason. Unfortunately, no one can trust anyone. I am at least fortunate that he is a good, compassionate person.

The enhancer said with empathy, "Here is your three-month supply of medicine. Please take one pill daily. Please avoid taking over one a day. If you still have nightmares, please come to investigate me again immediately. Remember! You are a devoted soldier to the STATE. You live for the glory of the STATE. LONG LIVE THE STATE!"

Investigator Hephaestus said, "Thank you! Since you, enhancer, are IN SERVICE TO THE GREAT STATE, I brought you forbidden steak and potatoes. We do not know where the forbidden food came from. I need to leave now and will see you in three months. Ensure that you cease laboring in six hours. LONG LIVE THE STATE!"

The investigator left and Aphrodite entered the room after waiting a few more minutes. Aphrodite said jokingly, "Of course, you are going to share the forbidden food with me? I will get some drinks."

Aristides responded, "Of course I shall share! Please set the timer for five hours and thirty minutes. We need to be done by then. We must be in our domicile in six hours. I do not wish to deal with another guardian, vanguard, or investigator. We, unfortunately, need approximately four hours for all the uploads. I am almost finished with the operations required prior to starting the upload."

Aphrodite went and returned with some drinks. She carefully prepared a table with plates and silverware for their highly unusual meal. The enhancer continued to ply diligently.

He stated with delight, "We can download now!" The enhancer attached a computer cord to the back of Solon's neck, which was hooked up to a sophisticated computer with the latest upgrades and technology. Moreover, the enhancer had invented and created the remarkably sophisticated computer.

Aristides smiled and spoke. "Well, it is time to dine! The download will take four hours. This will provide one hour left to walk to our home." Aristides took a stool at the simple table that Aphrodite had prepared with a flower in the center. Aphrodite arose and placed a kiss on Aristides' right cheek; then, she took half of his potato. He smiled and gave her half of his steak.

They lowered their heads and prepared to pray. Aphrodite spoke reverently. "Lord, thank you for giving us Solon, as well as this wonderful meal. Thank you for having Aristides in my life."

Aristides rejoiced, "Amen!"

Aphrodite said, "You were very kind and respectful toward the investigator."

He replied, "We must show compassion, love, and forgiveness toward all, even our potential enemies and adversaries. Moreover, Investigator Hephaestus has seen a tremendous amount of evil and terror that few men could ever endure.

"He does not know this, but I am the one that fought to save his life. The cold-hearted STATE wanted to execute him since it was determined to be cost prohibitive for the ALL-KNOWING STATE. I responded to the ELITE that I could do all the operations and artificial limbs under their estimate. In addition, I argued that I was developing a new procedure that needed to be tested for combat injuries. The ELITES granted me permission, and they insisted that I had better be successful. By the grace of God, I succeeded."

Aphrodite said inquisitively, "What was the new procedure?"

He declared, "The new procedure for the authoritarian STATE is to show compassion, love, and forgiveness to all. This must occur especially toward their citizens and honorable soldiers. We are all divine sovereign individuals and God's children."

She spoke, "This is true! We are all divine, sovereign individuals. By the way, that means you had the assistance from your first AI specialist. Is this true?"

Aristides laughed and stated, "Of course, this is correct! However, you are prettier and I truly trust you and love you!

"By the way, in about a few hours, you need to turn on AI Thirteen and give him instructions to monitor Solon in this room all night. We shall return at 7:00 a.m. tomorrow. Tell AI Thirteen that Solon should not be disturbed until 6:00 a.m. Solon will be extremely hungry and thirsty when he wakes up. Ensure that he has at least three days of nutritional substances consumed by the time we arrive. The good nutritional substances are in the refrigerator."

Aphrodite responded, "Yes, you are correct. I am prettier. Do not forget it. By the way, what are Solon's uploads?"

Aristides replied, "Oh, all the uploads for a soldier and military officer, as well as a guardian or vanguard, as you stated earlier. I uploaded some forbidden uploads like the bible, the US

Constitution, and world history. I uploaded some great philosophy books from Dostoevsky, Immanuel Kant, René Descartes, and others.

"Some uploads are only available when danger is detected, such as martial arts and karate. In addition, he will be aware what uploads and knowledge are STATE forbidden to avoid detection. Finally, I installed a device in him that will prevent the STATE from discovering forbidden files."

Aphrodite smiled and spoke. "That is excellent!" After they finished eating, they went back to work.

Aristides was an exceptional and well-respected enhancer since he enhanced humans to be soldiers or officers. In addition, he had medically assisted ELITES and vanguards. However, other enhancers generally specialized in only one classification. For example, the second classification had the least downloads and few enhancements. Their life expectancy rarely exceeded thirty-six years. Furthermore, there were built-in health issues that ensured natural death by forty years of age. Their downloads rarely exceeded their purpose. In other words, if you were a repairer, you only were downloaded the info for a particular machine and nothing else. This classification was clearly being reduced. Furthermore, this classification was being replaced by AI specialists and sophisticated robots.

Later, after approximately three hours, Aphrodite turned on AI Thirteen and gave him the instruction. AI Thirteen went to the other room and monitored Solon. She sent a message to the higher headquarters informing them of their current progress. Aphrodite and Aristides looked at each other with the realization that they were done for this exhausting day.

The enhancer looked at AI Thirteen. "See you tomorrow at 7:00 a.m. Goodnight!"

They left the office and headed for their domicile. As they cautiously were walking home, they saw a deprived and poor laborer along the sidewalk. The laborer recognized them and immediately moved out of the way. The laborer was scared to make eye contact. She shook in absolute fear.

Aristides said pleasantly, "Good evening!"

The laborer avoided making eye contact and bowed toward Aristides. "Guardian sir, good evening. I am not worthy to be in your presence."

The laborer pondered to herself, *Is this a good, caring guardian or an evil one? I do not know. I know that my existence means nothing to many, especially the ELITE. The last enhancer assaulted me and called me a useless laborer. I am deeply scared of all of them.*

Aristides said, "Thank you for your devoted service to the GREAT STATE!"

The laborer gasped. *Thank goodness!* The laborer looked up, clothed in her dirty, raggedy outfit, which clearly should be replaced. She expressed delightfully, "Thank you, kind guardian! Have a wonderful evening! May the STATE bless you!"

3

DAY 3: THE PHYSICAL ENHANCEMENTS

AT THEIR DOMICILE, Aphrodite prepared breakfast, which was cereal, toast, and bacon. In addition, she prepared a couple cups of coffee. She was also listening to the televised daily propaganda called UTOPIAN NEWS, which was the only approved broadcast. Today, like most days, the advertising media discussed how wonderful the ELITES were and the greatness of the STATE. The media reminded repeatedly that we were winning the endless war against the Aztec Empire. Of course, the media marketed STATE products or services that all citizens should consume and obtain by STATE credit. All STATE credit was regulated, controlled, and time sensitive.

After Aristides completed his shower and dressed, he entered the room and gave a hug and a kiss to Aphrodite. She then turned on a security device that blocked all monitoring within their domicile.

Aphrodite stood in the middle of the kitchen and admired their cozy, petite place. She thought to herself, ***Since Aristides is a guardian, he is allowed an AI robot, and, of course, I am pretending to be one.***

All guardians' residences were comprised of five rooms: a small kitchen, a bedroom, a tiny office, a bathroom, and a living room. All five rooms had either shelves or closets, but no windows. The total square footage was approximately eight hundred square feet; however, in the living room there was one wall with a large mirror, which made the room appear grander. All the rooms were painted gold to match their classification.

Aphrodite thought, *I wish that it was painted white; however, Aristides is pleased that I am able to keep the petite dwelling spotless and orderly for both of us. I am delighted that Aristides regularly compliments me on my exceptional feminine touch. He frequently states that I am extremely meticulous, and he believes I make the cozy place appealing and gorgeous. Besides, he ensures that I always have at least one flower, which is normally on the kitchen table.*

However, I wish that I could do something about the unbearable outside. We do not have a lawn or a backyard. Our neighborhood is dreadful. The outside is ubiquitously deprived of art, nature, and beauty.

Aphrodite smiled and joked, "Well, are you wearing authorized gold outfit one, two, or three?"

Aristides replied, "It is outfit number three, which is the same as one and two. I look the same every day!"

She joked, "That is great! I am also wearing outfit number three, which is the same as one and two."

He replied, "Love, at least you make your outfit look marvelous and beautiful!"

Aphrodite beamed and replied, "Let us say grace."

She prayed aloud, *"Let us thank Almighty God, maker of heaven and earth, for our second nutritious meal in a row. May God bless this meal and let us continue to commit treason in His Glorious Name."*

Aristides prayed, *"Lord, please keep Solon in the palms of Your Hands and prepare Solon for Your glory and to do Your Will. Please give mercy and comfort to Investigator Hephaestus. Lord, please forgive us for our sins and give us wisdom to do*

Your will. As revealed in Psalm 23: 'Yea, though I walk through the shadow of death, I fear no evil: for thou art with me; thy rod and thy staff, they comfort me.' Amen."

Aristides expressed, "Well, parts of this meal are genuine."

Aphrodite said inquisitively, "Why did you say that?"

He replied, "The GREAT STATE does not allow anyone except the ELITE, the military, and classification four to have genuine food for each meal. The meat that we receive is made from insects. However, the fruits and vegetables are still genuine for us and classification three. The second classification laborers and technician souls, unfortunately, are fed synthetic food. These synthetic foods include the fruits and vegetables that are chemically made and are not naturally grown. This is why they suffer from obesity, diabetes, and other health issues. Eighty percent of the second classification souls are obese. Fortunately, the good news for the first classification soldier is that they are required to eat healthy and are physically active because of being in combat constantly. Of course, the GREAT STATE guarantees that the soldiers are fed properly to secure that they are fit killing machines.

"The STATE claimed to reduce the world's carbon footprint, so laborers and others were not authorized to eat meat. Since I am a guardian, you and I can avoid synthetic foods and get our fourteen-meal allotment per week."

Aphrodite said with a tender smile, "Well, that is not something I like to hear in the morning while eating breakfast. Love, you can have my insect bacon. I am not an insectivorous. By the way, we need to understand how to grow our own food."

Aristides took her artificial bacon and ate it. He replied, "I have already started. I will show you later, love. We are going to have an extremely busy day again."

They finished getting ready. Aphrodite turned off the security device, and they left together for the medical room.

Back where Solon and AI Thirteen were, AI Thirteen prepared three meals for Solon. The meals were high-calorie protein drinks with a strawberry flavor and were dark liquid crimson in color. He obtained a red physical fitness outfit for Solon.

While AI Thirteen was working, Solon woke up; however, he kept his eyes closed. Solon thought to himself, *I had a strange dream last night. Well, I think it was a dream, since it may have been the first time that I slept and dreamt. I do not recall ever dreaming before; however, I think that I have slept before.*

This dream was so vivid to me. The dream seemed to be related to what I was struggling with and questioning. What am I? Who am I? What am I becoming?

This existential dream began with me as a robot with anatomical characteristics. In the dream, I was just activated. In this profound dream, my robotic consciousness was just for one day, or probably for a relatively short amount of time. Moreover, I still do not really understand what time is. Next, I dreamt that a kind enhancer told me to lie on a bed and he turned me off. The humane enhancer with his lovely AI specialist commenced to download data and information into my synthetic hardware. After some time, the caring enhancer told me to wake up in my dream. When I woke up in my dream, I was a human and no longer a robot. I was a human with downloaded information with no experiences related to this information. I was confused in the dream and questioned my identity. Am I a robot becoming human or have I always been a human that thought I used to be a robot?

AI Thirteen went to where Solon was sleeping. He gently shook the medical bed. AI Thirteen stated, "It is time to arise. Please drink the three red protein drinks on the table."

Solon, who was extremely hungry, eagerly went and drank with little hesitation.

AI Thirteen informed, "Your STATE-approved name is Solon. I shall henceforth call you Solon. Solon, please take a shower. The enhancer should be here in approximately fifty minutes." AI Thirteen gave him his clothes. Solon headed to the shower. After approximately thirty minutes, he came out of the shower room fully dressed.

AI Thirteen happily stated, "Outstanding, you have clothed yourself properly with approximately twenty minutes to spare."

Solon expressed, "Thanks! However, I am still hungry."

AI Thirteen replied, "I am sorry. You must wait for the enhancer, since he only allowed three drinks."

At that moment, enhancer Aristides and Aphrodite entered the room. The enhancer said, "Solon, you look well. Are you still hungry?"

Solon responded, "I am famished!"

Aphrodite went to prepare the additional drinks. Aristides said, "Solon, please lay on the medically enhanced bed."

Aphrodite returned with three drinks. Solon immediately guzzled them down. After she injected a shot into his arm, he went to sleep. She then went around AI Thirteen and turned him off. She then ensured that the room was secured. Aphrodite joked, "It is time to commit treason!"

Aristides said, "Love, of course we shall commit treason! I am going to enhance Solon's arms to twice the muscle mass of a chimpanzee's arms. We want him to retain the human advantage of being able to swim in water and maintain the human endurance of a long-distance runner. As you are aware, chimpanzees cannot swim because their body's muscle density causes them to sink to the bottom like a rock.

"I shall improve his athletic abilities and endurance to the equivalence of an Olympic athlete from the twenty-first century. He will run under a four-minute mile and have the endurance to run a marathon plus.

"My biggest concern is that his body structure will require a high daily calorie intake. This is clearly his Achilles' heel and vulnerability. His body fat will be very low. He could starve to death in a couple of weeks without food, or at least he will suffer severe malnutrition. Aphrodite, I believe that this initial physical upgrade will take approximately five hours to be accomplished."

As Aphrodite was searching on Aristides' computer, she saw a picture of Aristides' first son. Aphrodite questioned, "Dear, I found a picture of your first son who looks very similar to Solon. Out of curiosity, whatever happened to your first son?"

He replied, "Dear, please come here and assist me and I shall tell you what I know or I am aware of." She immediately came over and assisted him.

Aristides took a deep breath and stated, "My first son's name is Moros, which was a name given by the Vanguard Hades. Vanguard Hades reports to ELITE Seth who is a satanist. Moros started under my care, and I did the initial upload for a soldier and a military officer. Unfortunately, I gave him the upload of books on Nazism and Marxism with no other books to assist him. I had already done some physical enhancements that improved his endurance and strength.

"ELITE Seth came to see me and ordered me to the front line to help in the war effort. The ELITE Seth ordered Vanguard Hades to complete Moros' enhanced transformation to a soldier. Hades probably discovered that Moros was improved and could be an officer.

"Vanguard Hades killed specialist Hestia. He probably wanted to complete the procedure with no witnesses. Moros became an officer. For the last two years, he has been in the last two Gladiator events for the annual Martius Festival in March. Moros was victorious in his gladiator events both years. Last year, he was awarded the silver gladiator badge.

"I believe that he has completed over three years in combat and he has advanced in the officer ranks rather rapidly. He is now a lieutenant colonel. Furthermore, he was awarded a heroic medal for killing his commander, who was deemed to be a coward. Moreover, Moros was victorious in the same battle during which he murdered his commander.

"Regarding Vanguard Hades, he is on track to be an ELITE. Vanguard Hades is a devoted, materialistic, satanic Marxist who is driven to establish his version of a utopia. Of course, this is at the sacrifice of the current poor and others. He desires greatness at all costs. He strives to be an Uber Mensch and only cares about obtaining power. Moros is probably the same.

"Hades loathes weakness and femininity. He loathes any arguments or actions that lead to good. Hades, unlike some

ELITES, will show no mercy toward anyone who holds a belief in God. There are some ELITES, probably over forty percent and mostly atheists, who will look the other way regarding people believing in religion or God. As long as that belief is not directed against the STATE, these ELITES will tolerate it.

"However, Vanguard Hades tolerates nothing he identifies as a weakness. This is probably an additional reason for murdering Hestia.

"By the way, Hestia was a typical AI specialist. She assisted me by using a stolen egg that was fertilized with my semen. We implanted the fertilized egg in a STATE-approved womb and later transported it to an incubator. She, of course, is not like you since you are a genuine AE woman who is pretending to be an AI specialist. Love, as you are aware, we did the same procedure for Solon who is a product of your egg and my semen."

Aphrodite laughed and expressed, "Correction! I am not pretending to be a specialist. I take my vocation very seriously! By the way, I shall always love you and be thankful for you for saving my life!"

Aristides responded, "Please thank Captain Hypnos, who brought you to me when you were seriously injured in a battle against the Aztec Empire. He must have respected life and civilians. Unfortunately, he died in the next battle.

"Fortunately for us, there were so many casualties and deaths from this deadly battle that it was easy for me to conceal your identity. Our empire does not have the identity of others from another empire like the Aztec Empire, especially civilians. There was a severely damaged AI robot that Captain Hypnos asked me to repair and take under my wing. Aphrodite, your

AI robot identity is from the AI robot that Captain Hypnos brought to me."

Aphrodite smiled and expressed, "**Gracias!** You know you are sleeping with the enemy! My amour, I love you!"

Aristides responded, "I love you too!"

She informed, "In the Aztec Empire, the Christian and Catholic faiths are still very strong and dominant. However, they practice in complete secrecy. The resistance to the Aztec Empire's ELITES is growing stronger and stronger each day. There has been a significant increase in the number of religious martyrs in the last couple of years; however, that just boosts our resolve and motivates us to resist.

"I promise to you and God that I will resist this tyranny to my last dying breath!"

He responded, "We shall resist them together. Unfortunately, ever since the eight empires and GLUE have adopted Leninism, the ELITES have made the lives of their civilians significantly worse. Hell was not good enough. They wanted a complete Dante's *Inferno*. Their Lenin political philosophy has amplified the suffering for all, even for themselves. Leninism has no tolerance for any view counter to the STATE. All religions and beliefs that question the STATE are crushed by the oppressive boot of the STATE. Of course, the STATE is treated as the only accepted true religion and dogma—except for the satanists."

Aphrodite asked, "Why would you say the suffering has increased even for the ELITE?"

Aristides responded, "To be a tyrant is like a dictator riding a man-eating tiger. You know if you fall off, the carnivorous and famished tiger will devour you. The citizens of all the empires will pounce at any opportunity to overthrow the ELITE, especially if they demonstrate any form of weakness. Every year, several ELITES and vanguards are assassinated by the rebels, but the fake STATE media conceals and hides the murderous events. Unfortunately, the fake STATE media protects the propaganda by only announcing that the citizens are satisfied with their overlords. Of course, the deceitful messages will express that the ELITE adore their citizens and will strive to create a utopia in their empire and the world.

"The ELITES' actions reveal they are convinced that we are all stupid and gullible. Fortunately for us, the ELITES clearly underestimate the will and abilities of the citizens of their empire.

"By the way, in approximately fifteen minutes, Solon will be ready to be awakened. Love, please prepare several protein drinks for Solon. He will be famished and dehydrated. Please prepare several glasses of water as well."

Aphrodite left and headed to the adjacent room. He continued to work diligently on Solon. After several minutes, she entered the room. Aristides gently woke up Solon. Aphrodite assisted Solon as he raised himself up in the bed. She handed Solon a drink, and he inhaled it. She immediately gave him another one, which resulted in the same reaction.

Aristides said, "Solon, please slowly get out of bed and stand up." Solon complied slowly. The enhancer examined him medically. Aphrodite came over and drew some blood from him. Next, she injected some drugs into him in order to reduce his pain and swelling from the procedures.

He requested, "Solon, please go on the treadmill and start walking. You will continue walking until it reads eight miles or you collapse from exhaustion. If you are motivated, you may run.

However, if you decide to run, imagine in your mind an exceptional runner with an excellent running form and technique."

Solon imagined a historic Olympian runner during a time when that person broke the historic four-minute mile. Solon ran, but he stumbled and his form was not very good.

Aristides commanded, "Please stop. Solon, it is not your fault. This is the first time that you have ever run. Please imagine a proper running form and start again." Solon started running again and fast; however, his upper body was not relaxed.

Aristides expressed, "Solon, please stop again! You need to relax your upper body while you run. You are clearly doing better. Please imagine again a proper form. We need to improve your muscle memory. One positive: Your running endurance is exceptional! We just need to get your form correct. Please start again."

This happened for several additional occurrences until Solon achieved a proper running form. Finally, he was ready to perform the eight-mile run.

Solon started running properly with a dedicated perfunctory pace for one mile with a consistent six-minute pace. After completing two miles, he accelerated to a five-minute pace. After forty-four minutes and eight seconds, he completed the event.

Aristides smiled and expressed, "That was excellent! You broke the record by approximately two minutes. In two days, we will do this again, and I want you to be under thirty-five minutes. Solon, please go to the punching bag machine. I want you to punch the bag five times with each hand. Before doing so, conceive the proper boxing technique, which is in your mind. Before punching, play in your mind the sequence of a boxer who has excellent form and techniques."

Solon closed his eyes and imagined a great professional boxer punching another heavyweight boxer. His first punch was with his right, then his second with his left. He did those punches four more times.

Aristides advised, "You must improve your technique. It is not bad for your first time. You need to improve the placement of your feet and your stance. Imagine again a proper punch. Try it again with both hands five times."

Solon imagined again the proper punching technique and started punching. Aristides interrupted him several more times until Solon performed the punches properly.

Aristides smiled from ear to ear and stated proudly, "Both hands averaged over one thousand psi, one thousand and eight psi for the right hand and one thousand and eighty psi for the left. That also breaks the record for the first day and exceeds a historical heavyweight professional boxer. In two days, I want you to exceed thirteen hundred psi. Please remember that you need to practice improving your muscle memory.

"Aphrodite, please give him some well-deserved additional drinks. Solon, so far, you have already exceeded the physical requirements to be considered an officer. Keep this up, and you may be considered for being a first lieutenant, which is the highest direct commission."

Aphrodite handed Solon two protein drinks. He gulped them down and said appreciatively, "Aphrodite, thank you! I deeply appreciate your kindness." She smiled with gratitude.

Aristides informed, "Solon, for your final physical event for today, please go to the weight machine. The weight machine is set for one thousand pounds. I want you to imagine an Olympic weightlifter lifting weights over his head. You may do up to three lifts. The next will be increased by one hundred pounds, as well as the next. In other words, the second one is at eleven hundred pounds and the third is at twelve hundred pounds."

Solon closed his eyes and imagined a historic Olympic weightlifter when the Olympian won the gold medal. He imagined these exceptional techniques in his mind. Solon started doing his first lift, but he struggled with the proper form and technique.

Aristides commanded, "Please stop! You need to squat lower and improve your technique. You are close. Please try again." Aristides stopped Solon several times; however, Solon eventually figured it out. He then did his three lifts with ease and with proper form and technique.

Aristides smiled like an extremely proud father. "You broke the record again with a maximum lift of twelve hundred pounds! In two days, I want you to do fifteen hundred pounds.

"I want to guide you with a critical piece of advice. This will separate you from the lion's share of soldiers and officers. I have downloaded in you a tremendous amount of information. However, that does not mean that your body has gained the muscle memory. You need to practice in physical motion in order for your body to acquire muscle memory. On a very positive note, when I interrupted you when you were doing the physical activity improperly, you immediately listened and adjusted. In addition, you imagined the physical activity correctly. All the downloads in your head must be practiced in order to form proper muscle memory.

"For example, I have downloaded in you several martial arts like karate. However, you must show and perform karate to acquire the muscle memory, such as practicing a roundhouse kick. Solon, do you understand me?"

Solon responded, "Yes, sir! Guardian, I understand. I shall do as you advised."

Aphrodite came back, and she joked, "There are clearly no concerns from the blood draw. He is as healthy as a horse with the strength of a gorilla and the speed of a gazelle. Aristides, I am going to turn on AI Thirteen. Please give him his instructions." Aphrodite left the room, turned on AI Thirteen, and they both came back into the room.

Aristides instructed, "We shall return at seven a.m. tomorrow. AI Thirteen, do not disturb Solon until six a.m. Solon will be extremely hungry and thirsty again when he wakes up. Ensure that he has at least three days of nutritional substances consumed by the moment we arrive. You may give one or two more drinks if Solon requests them. The good nutritional substances are in the refrigerator. Solon, please shower and wear a clean red PT outfit. Well, have a good night's sleep. See you tomorrow."

They left the office and headed for their domicile, taking the same direction as they had last night. The route, like seemingly everywhere, was dreadful. There were no lovely plants or art or attractiveness. Everything was a dreadful gray color; however, it was clean and orderly. Everything was maintained and created to be purely functional without any beauty. The unpleasant city was a creative architect's nightmare, as it had clearly been created by a psychotic, cold, functionality-motivated engineer. As they were walking home, they saw the same peasant laborer on the same sidewalk. The laborer recognized them and moved out of the way.

The laborer thought to herself, *Great! I believe that this is the same pleasant guardian from last night.* The laborer reluctantly made eye contact and smiled. She said respectfully, "Sir guardian and AI specialist, good evening!"

Aristides said pleasantly, "Good evening! Thank you again for your devoted service to the GREAT STATE!"

The laborer raised her head with confidence and smiled with delight and respect. She replied, "Thank you, kind guardian! Have a wonderful evening! May the STATE bless you with honor!"

4

DAY 4: THE PHYSICAL AND MENTAL TESTS

AS SOLON WAS RESTING IN THE RECOVERY BED, he was pondering and reflecting intensively. *I feel as if the EMPIRE has downloaded me like a soulless computer with information and data that I have clearly not experienced or lived. I am only a few days old with thoughts and occurrences of my own. With my limited experience, I believe humans did not gain information and data this way for their entire existence and evolution.*

According to several of my historical downloads, humans learned from families, parents, neighbors, and educational institutions. AI Thirteen has already expressed that the GREAT STATE has deemed families and parents as inefficient and undesirable. Hence, without a doubt, families and parents existed in the past, even if I have not experienced them yet.

However, I have no mother or father or family either. I have no friends or companions. AI Thirteen is clearly none of these. On the contrary, he was polite and respectful to me yesterday.

I like to believe that the Enhancer and the AI specialist care about me; conversely, that is probably a dream or merely a yearning. They may just be performing the will of the STATE like AI Thirteen. Given these thoughts, I feel completely alone and confused.

The enhancer advised me that I have had a cornucopia of information downloaded. This does not mean that my body has achieved the muscle memory, especially regarding martial arts. I need to practice these physical activities in order for my body to gain muscle memory. Thus, the GREAT STATE has sacrificed ancient learning practices, like experiences, for the efficiency of speedy download. Was this a good idea as well as good for the individual? I think that the enhancer's excellent advice about muscle memory proves that learning through experience is critical. The state abandoned the time to acquire muscle memory or does not see the need; thus, the STATE is in error or does not care.

AI Thirteen stated that I am at the maturity level and physically at the age of an eighteen-year-old ancient human. What does that mean? It means that humans normally took eighteen years to get to my development. Perhaps I am missing and have been deprived of eighteen critical years of experiences, thoughts, and dreams. Why would the supposed GREAT STATE deem that it is necessary for me to be denied these eighteen years of development? Was it that inefficient? Are there other sacrifices that the GREAT STATE deemed inefficient?

AI Thirteen stated that I am STATE property and my self-interest does not matter. I am developing into a first classification, an enlisted soldier. I believe that I am another expendable soldier for the GREAT STATE and the current endless war. There is a high probability that I will not survive that long since I will be in combat for at least four years.

According to my downloads, there were babies, children, and teenagers. I have witnessed no babies or children. However, they may still exist and I should continue searching for them.

My download informs me that there were institutions like schools, universities, museums, churches, parks, gymnasiums, *libraries, and other institutions that existed to gain knowledge and the arts. I have experienced none of the arts, like paintings or music or poetry or games or athletic competition in sports. I have seen none of these institutions. However, I may experience this later since I must remind myself that I am only a few days old.*

However, why should I trust the downloaded information? The supposed GREAT STATE downloaded information could be issued to me to keep me hoping and striving for something better. The downloads are there to keep me amused or confused and possibly deceived. Since I shall be a soldier, my purpose may be to fight for the empire and the people to have a better life, a life with less suffering and hopelessness. I do not know. I must continue to assess and maintain an open mind.

At their domicile, Aphrodite was dressed for work and she was in the kitchen. Aphrodite was preparing their favorite breakfast, which was pancakes with strawberries and blueberries. Furthermore, she prepared a couple of cups of tea. After Aristides completed his shower, he entered the room and gave a hug and a kiss to her. She then turned on the security device that blocked all monitoring within their domicile, which was clearly their daily routine. Aristides came in and sat.

They heard something at the door. Aristides turned off the security system and answered the door. There were two vanguards, present for their monthly inspection. The intimidating and ruthless vanguards entered and verified the couples' identification by reading their biometric ID in their right hands. They quickly inspected the house for contraband and unauthorized personnel. After fifteen minutes of an intrusive inspection, one vanguard declared, "Guardian enhancer and AI specialist Aphrodite, you passed your inspection with no STATE violations. Remember to watch and adhere to updates on **UTOPIA NEWS, The State News that Cares.** HAIL TO THE GREAT STATE! Carry on!" The vanguards quickly departed, and Aristides turned on the security system.

Aphrodite stated sarcastically, "Well, great, we passed again! I cannot wait until the next unscheduled invasive inspection to protect that we remain in terror!"

Aristides expressed, "Love, I am sorry! At least we were not discovered again. Let us say grace and eat."

They bowed their heads and prepared to pray. Aristides prayed, *"Lord, please keep Solon in the palm of Your Hands and prepare Solon for Your glory to do Your Will. In addition, please give mercy and comfort to all in this sinful world, even for the godless ELITE and vanguards. God, please help us all to find Your love and glorious purpose.*

"As it is revealed in 1 Corinthians 16:13, 'Be on your guard; stand firm in the faith; be courageous; be strong. Also, as revealed in Mathew 6:14: 'For if ye forgive men their trespasses, your heavenly Father will also forgive you.'"

Aristides expressed, "Well, it is our favorite meal that was made from your loving care. This meal has no insects from the STATE."

They finished eating, and then they finished getting ready for another long day. Aphrodite gave him a kiss, then she turned off the security device. They left their domicile for the medical room.

Back where Solon was, AI Thirteen stood up in order to wake up Solon. He gently shook the bed and Solon woke up. AI Thirteen said with kindness, "Good morning! Please drink the three red protein beverages on the table." Solon, who was extremely hungry, eagerly went and drank the three protein drinks with little hesitation.

AI Thirteen requested, "Solon, please take a shower. The enhancer should be here in approximately forty-five minutes." AI Thirteen gave Solon his clothes. After approximately twenty minutes, Solon came out of the shower room fully dressed.

Solon responded, "AI Thirteen, I am still ravenous. May I have another protein drink?"

AI Thirteen replied, "Yes, here are two additional drinks."

Solon gulped down the two beverages. Solon stated, "AI Thirteen, thank you! I appreciate your assistance. You have been very kind!"

AI Thirteen replied, "You're welcome!"

A few minutes later, the Enhancer and Aphrodite arrived. The Enhancer inquired, "Solon, you look better than yesterday. Are you still hungry?"

Solon responded, "No, thank you. I have had plenty."

Aphrodite went and turned off AI Thirteen.

Solon asked, "Would you please answer some questions for me?"

Aristides looked at Aphrodite, and she understood what he wanted. Aristides responded, "Yes!"

Solon questioned, "Who or what am I? What am I becoming?"

Aristides was amazed by his inquisitiveness. The enhancer informed, "You are a biological human with some biological enhancements and artificial intelligence enhancements. My goal is for you to remain human and not lose your humanity and nature.

"I completely understand that you would not trust us. If I were you, I would not trust us either. However, Aphrodite and I are the only ones that currently care for you, which is easier to say than to demonstrate. Our evidence for you is that Aphrodite will continue to reprogram AI Thirteen to care for you. Please understand that AI Thirteen cannot witness anything contrary to the STATE. It is not because AI Thirteen will betray you; it is because the STATE can retrieve data and video logs from an AI robot since they record everything while activated."

Solon asked, "Well, what about Aphrodite? How can we trust AI specialist Aphrodite?"

Aphrodite said sincerely, "I am an AE HUMAN, like the enhancer. Therefore, I am not an AI robot. Delightfully, I am your biological mother, but we have to keep this a secret; otherwise, we all shall be executed for treason against the STATE. In addition, the enhancer, who I love, is your biological father. He saved my life, and he was able to conceal my identity. I know that this must be overwhelming for you. I am sorry!"

Aristides expressed, "Well, the cat is out of the bag. Solon, we have a tremendous amount of work to accomplish. I promise you that I will prepare you to be an exceptional military officer as well as reveal and inform to you all that you should know. I only ask that you keep this among us."

Solon articulated with sincerity, "I shall keep our family secrets. Besides, I am delighted that I have a mom and a dad. In my brief existence, I have felt so utterly alone, deprived, and confused. This is the best news that I have heard! By the way, I have noticed that AI Thirteen is being nicer to me."

The enhancer expressed, "We are happy that you are delighted that we are your parents. Aphrodite has done an excellent job reprograming AI Thirteen. Please be aware that he will love flowers, which will be a great clue that the reprograming and transformation are complete.

"I am sorry to tell you that we do not have a tremendous amount of time to prepare you; but we promise to perform our best. First, we need to get you ready for the final physical test and cognitive test for acceptance as an officer. This will allow us three additional days of preparation. The good news is that the cognitive test is basic questions from math to official language skills. However, the test has some traps that prevent most soldiers from scoring eighty-five or higher.

"Aphrodite, please contact headquarters and request a test proctor to be here in several hours. Solon, the test proctor will bring a laptop, and you will need to answer the basic questions on the laptop. If you score eighty-five or higher, then you met the first requirement to be an officer. You will have an hour to complete the test.

"In addition, Aphrodite, please arrange for the physical fitness test, which comprises push-ups, sit-ups, and a three-mile run.

"Solon, for the push-up test, you will have three minutes to perform as many push-ups as you can. For the sit-up test, you will have three minutes to perform as many push-ups as you can. You need to do over sixty-six push-ups and over sixty-six sit-ups. In addition, for the three-mile run, you need to complete it under eighteen minutes. I am not concerned about the three-mile run. You are very prepared for this event. However, we must have you prepare for the other two events, tests.

"Solon, please imagine performing a proper push-up and proper sit-up. Now, please go to the mat and perform sixty-six of each."

Solon went to the mat and performed the push-up event. Solon struggled to do a proper push-up. His form was not terrible, but it was clearly unacceptable.

Aristides demanded, "Please halt! Relax and imagine a proper push-up again. You need to develop muscle memory. Your strength and endurance are excellent; however, your muscles need to learn the correct form." The enhancer told Solon a few more times to stop until Solon did the push-up test properly.

Solon started doing the proper push-up event again. After sixty-six push-ups, he started doing the sit-up test. Aristides insisted once again, "Please stop, again! Take it easy and imagine doing a proper sit-up and perform it slowly and accurately. Again, you need to develop muscle memory. You clearly have the endurance." The enhancer told Solon several more times to stop until Solon did the sit-up event properly. Solon went to the mat and performed the proper sit-up event.

Aristides expressed, "Great! Now, please perform sixty-six of each again." Solon did the push-up and sit-up events properly, as well as within time.

Aphrodite came back and stated that the test proctor was coming in five hours. He wanted Solon to do the physical fitness test here right after the cognitive test. Aphrodite took AI Thirteen to the other room to charge.

Aristides expressed, "Solon, you are ready for the fitness test. I need to get you ready for the cognitive test. I will start with some basic math questions in order to test your memory recall. Here are five basic math operations:"

1. What is five plus fifteen?
2. What is thirty-eight minus twenty-eight?
3. What is eight times five?
4. What is twelve divided by six?
5. What is ten squared?

Solon answered, "These answers are twenty, ten, forty, two, and one hundred."

Aristides responded, "Correct! Your mathematical operational recall is excellent. Now I am going to give you a harder type of math problem, and I am going to write the equation on the board with the following three answers:"

$3X+10=40$
A) 10
B) 12
C) 14

Solon answered, "The answer is 'A.'"

Aristides responded, "Excellent! Your recall of basic algebra works well. Now I am going to give you the hardest type of math problem, and I am going to write the equation on the board again with the following three answers:"

$X^2+10=110$
A) 10
B) 14

C) -10 and 10

Solon answered, "The answer is 'A' again."

Aristides responded, "Solon, you fell for the trap. The answer is 'C,' since both ten and negative ten are the correct answer. This is not your fault. These are the first math problems that you have performed. The weakness of the download is that people look at the first download and answer that is relevant. Take your time and look at all the answers. You need to pick the best answer. We shall try one more to emphasize this point.

"Now I am going to give you another of the hardest type of math problem:"

$$4X^2 + 10 = 26$$

A) 2

B) 10 and -10

C) -2 and 2

Solon answered, "The answer is 'C.'"

Aristides responded, "Outstanding! We will now perform some basic questions that you should know. For example, what color does the ELITE wear?"

A) Green

B) Black

C) Red

Solon answered, "The answer is 'B.'"

He reacted. "Fantastic! Here is another question. For example, what does the ELITE wear?"

A) Black

B) Silver necklace

C) Both A and B

Solon answered, "The answer is 'A.'"

Aristides advised, "Solon, you fell for the deception again. The answer is 'C' since it is a better answer. You must look at all the answers. Please avoid just finding the first accurate answer. This is a common mistake since you have not taken a multiple-choice test before. To do well on tests, you need the experience of taking tests and the experience of the test traps. You do not have any experience taking tests. Does this make sense to you so far?"

Solon responded, "Yes! Thank you! I will take my time and look at all the answers."

Aristides sincerely responded, "Great! You will perform well. Take your time, please. You could easily complete the test in thirty minutes; however, this might mean that you would probably fall for the tricks."

Solon, with the help of his father's tutoring, went over several other questions. Aristides explained all the potential test tricks and pitfalls. Solon was feeling confident, and he enjoyed working with his father.

They saw the warning light flashing at the door. Aphrodite went to answer the door and Test Proctor Titan, who was a guardian, entered the room.

The Test Proctor Titan spoke. **"HAIL TO THE GREAT STATE!** enhancer guardian Aristides and AI specialist, I am pleased that the potential soldier is ready to be tested. AI specialist Aphrodite mentioned to me that XY777-316, with the STATE-approved name of Solon, should be considered for potentially becoming an officer. AI specialists express exceptional advice and evaluations. I hope that this is the case. Besides, we need highly dedicated officers willing to serve and die in glory for the GREAT STATE. We shall start with the cognitive test."

The Test Proctor Guardian Titan started preparing his laptop. The Test Proctor Titan thought to himself, *Well, there will be one more for the meat grinder. Solon will be just cannon fodder. I bet that he will not last even a week as either a soldier or an officer. It does not matter. The ELITE are now pushing the death and body count before the March celebrations. I have advocated that the ELITE should just reduce the six-day training days to only three days. So far, they have rejected my sincere, excellent recommendation!*

Once the Test Proctor Guardian was prepared, Titan instructed, "Solon, sit here. You will have one hour to answer up to fifty questions. At the end of the test, you will see your result. You are not allowed any assistance on any question, and you may not leave until you are finished. There should only be one correct or best answer in each of the fifty multiple test questions. You may begin now. May the STATE assist you!"

After approximately forty-five minutes, Solon completed the test and looked at the Test Proctor Guardian. The Test Proctor Guardian Titan stated, "Solon, have you finished with the test?"

Solon replied, "Yes, and I know my score. I scored a ninety-eight."

The Test Proctor Guardian smiled and explained, "That is excellent! You have met the first requirement to be an officer. Moreover, you have tied with a few others with the highest score. You will have fifteen minutes to rest. I recommend that you use the lavatory."

When Solon returned, Test Proctor Guardian Titan instructed, "Solon, lay on this mat. You will start with a sit-up event, then go to a push-up event. You will have a maximum of six minutes to perform as many sit-ups and push-ups as physically possible; however, after three minutes, you must start performing the push-up event. Remember, you need to perform sixty-six proper sit-ups and sixty-six proper push-ups to meet the next officer requirement. For your information, you need to perform at least thirty of each to avoid being terminated. I am confident that this will not be a concern. Solon, you may begin." After approximately two minutes, he started the push-up event. After exactly four minutes, he stood upright, which ended the events.

The Test Proctor Guardian Titan expressed, "That was tremendous! You did 132 push-ups and 132 sit-ups, which is twice the officer requirement for these two events. In addition, you did this in only four minutes, which is exceptional! I believe that this may have broken the old record.

"Solon, you now will run for a distance of three miles on the treadmill. You must be under eighteen minutes for the officer requirement, which is a six-minute pace. In addition, you must complete the three miles under twenty-seven minutes to avoid being terminated. There is a timer and odometer on the treadmill to inform you of your progress. Since you are all set on the treadmill, you may begin."

Solon started running at an extremely fast pace. He completed the first mile in just under four minutes. He did just as well for the second mile. The third mile was extremely strong for him.

The Test Proctor Guardian Titan articulated in shock, "Unbelievable! Solon, your time is eleven minutes and forty-eight seconds, which is clearly a new record. You averaged three minutes and fifty-six seconds per mile. That is remarkable!

"You are now eligible to take the simulation combat test on day six of soldier training, as well as the other physical tests. If you pass the simulation test and the other physical tests, then you will have three additional days to be trained as an officer. These three days comprise your officer specialty course.

"I shall report this to headquarters and arrange for his simulation combat test and the other physical tests. Enhancer, great job and, of course, this will look fabulous on your record, as well. I shall leave now. **HAIL TO THE GREAT STATE!**"

Aristides replied, "Thank you! **HAIL TO THE GREAT STATE!**"

The Test Proctor Guardian Titan laughed to himself, *Another expendable jarhead for the endless GREAT STATE holy crusade!*

Aphrodite secured the door. Aphrodite worried to herself, *I am so afraid for Solon. I do not want to lose him. We must prepare him with exoteric skills and abilities.* Aphrodite tried to smile and expressed, "Solon, I am so proud of you! You did a great job!"

Solon replied, "Mom, I did it for you. I am delighted that you are proud of me. It clearly motivated me! Dad, could we discuss a few things?"

Aristides replied, "Of course! What would you like to discuss?"

Solon replied, "Dad, how did this all occur? How did we end up with the world being led by sixty-six tyrannical ELITES and eight thousand vanguards? I have been studying some of my historical downloads, and I'd like to hear from you what you think."

Aristides spoke thoughtfully, "Well, Solon, approximately eighty years ago, there was an artificial virus. This virus had several variants that the world leaders used to keep the people in total fear and under their control. The government leaders claimed that the virus was so contagious that everyone needed to be vaccinated by an experimental vaccine. Small businesses were forced to close in order to prevent the spread."

Solon innocently interrupted and stated, "According to my downloads, the world leaders and governments required everyone to stay home and small businesses to remain closed for a couple of weeks. Then, it turned into two plus years, which resulted in a plethora of small businesses closing permanently. However, many large global businesses profited billions of dollars and expanded their businesses. How could the leaders control the message?"

Aristides went into a detailed explanation. He expressed that the media was only reporting pro-vaccine information and suppressing any counter information that warned against using the experimental vaccine. He stated that large social media platforms canceled people's accounts if they stated any information counter to the pro-vaccine agenda. He emphasized that this was the case even if the person voiced medical concerns by a medically licensed doctor. Solon mentioned that this even occurred in the greatest superpower of the world; the United States was historically the home of the free and the home of the brave prior to the PLANDEMIC.

Aristides emphasized that you could not even argue the origin of the virus; the origin was eventually revealed, and it was determined that the virus came from a laboratory in the second-most powerful country of the world, China. This country was ruled by an authoritarian communist government.

Solon revealed that from his download, the government officials, even the United States government, claimed that there were no therapeutics or healthy lifestyle activities that existed to assist against the virus. He discussed that certain medical facts were suppressed, such as eighty percent of people who died from the virus were obese and had four or more morbidities or, on average, were over sixty-five years old. He also mentioned that the goalpost for regulations kept changing from month to month.

Solon asked, "Based on my historical download, there were two primary parties within the United States. What were their responses?"

Aristides responded with a protracted response. He stressed that One of the two political parties, democrats, pushed civil disturbance and violence to rioting; several cities had riots, arson, and vandalism that were under the political control of the democrats, which pushed defunding the police, as well as ceasing to protect the country's southern border. He also explained that the same party pressed for mail-in voting; mail-in voting brought about election corruption, as well as a massive reduction in election confidence. He did divulge that the other party, republicans, had traitors in it as well.

Solon discussed that prior to one presidential election in the United States, the media suppressed the information that was stored on a laptop; this laptop had incriminating information about illegal activity. This suppressed information clearly benefited the presidential candidate who allegedly won. Both agreed that the United States that led the world was clearly a house divided!

Solon stated that, according to his downloads, since several citizens lost their livelihoods or were working from home, the government determined that governmental assistance checks were required for them; the government was increasing expenditures with massive spending bills and printing additional money.

Aristides emphasized that the United States administration decided to go net zero carbon emissions, which meant a reduction in the use of fossil fuels, which was well over eighty percent of the energy used by its citizens.

Solon asked, "What about the rest of the world?"

Aristides explained that other nations were pushing the net zero agenda as well; the administration ended a pipeline to a neighboring friendly country, Canada. He stressed that the United States reduced domestic production of oil, which resulted in increased fuel prices, as well as increased prices for other goods and services; the agenda used faulty analysis that demonized fossil fuels, as well as nuclear power and hydroelectric power.

Solon responded that the supposed expert environmental advocates suppressed any disadvantages of technology like wind and solar; some disadvantages were the lack of reliability and other costs, such as needing backup and standby systems from other reliable energy sources like, ironically, fossil fuels when there was no wind or sun. Aristides explained that in the United States, this also resulted in inflation for all goods and services that probably exceeded over ten percent; however, previous methods of determining inflation rates would calculate the inflation rate nearly twice what the government reported.

Aristides claimed that in the Netherlands, which was the second food producer of the world, the government required their farmers to radically reduce their use of fertilizer. This resulted in several countries' farmers protesting their governments since a great number of farmers would lose their livelihood and farms.

Solon expressed that in another part of the world, a former world power, Russia, invaded a country that used to be part of its country, Ukraine. Ukraine's government was corrupt for having bioweapon production plants and was known for laundering money. Of course, the Ukraine's president took over the media and eliminated the opposition party of that country. The United States was sending large amounts of money to support the Ukraine's war effort. The United States president had a son who was rewarded millions from sitting on a Ukrainian oil company board, which the son was not qualified for. A United States intelligence agency suppressed the information and other incriminating evidence before a key presidential election. This suppressed information clearly led to the wrong person winning the election.

Aristides highlighted that the former president and presidential candidate in the next election was indicted for untested legal theory crimes and questioning the election results. The federal government raided his home because of alleged possession of classified documents. With a perspective of neo-McCarthyism, the full weight of the federal government was after this former president and presidential candidate. This resulted in over five trials and eventual conviction. The deep state eventually imprisoned the former president.

Aristides nodded in agreement and he responded, "We should not just focus on the eighty or so years ago, as there were events prior that led to these tragedies. There were numerous advocates for depopulation since the early 1900s. There was a world elitist forum that was in bed with world leaders and megacompanies to advocate depopulation and advocating a dictatorship form of world governance. This so-called economic forum advocated that you would own nothing and be happy. This, of course, revealed their true thoughts. Remember that Hitler wrote *Mein Kampf* before his reign of terror."

Aristides also expressed other historical examples that revealed deep state involvement, such as the use of deep energy weapons that destroyed areas that globalists wanted like Maui. After the media claimed climate fire, Maui was rebuilt as a globalist smart city with total surveillance and control of the people on the island.

Aristides stressed and reminded Solon that the incarcerated presidential candidate was the president in a previous term; however, his victory was obviously a black swan for the deep state and the people who truly pulled the strings, since they expected that their candidate could not lose. This clearly divided the country.

Solon asked, "What was happening in the nation that supposedly developed the virus?"

Aristides replied, "In China, their citizens were under severe dictatorial lockdowns and surveillance. These people had no rights since it was already a tyrannical Marxist country that established an Orwellian e-tyranny." In addition, Aristides explained that China implemented a social credit score system that controlled all economic and social activities of life. He continued to explain that Chinese citizens led a protest called the BLANK PAPER revolution, which resulted in the boot of the STATE coming to squish the protest; the tyrannical state lockdown was so severe that people were committing suicide to avoid poverty and starvation. He claimed that, obviously, the people were resisting being locked in their homes forever. China was clearly the blueprint and test case for globalists and elitists.

He revealed that what was difficult to recognize was that many country leaders were more concerned about global issues than their own country's matters. A significant number of state leaders had their true allegiance to unknown puppet masters, and they seemed to have no true loyalty to their own country. He emphasized that world leaders were not upholding their oath of office.

Solon replied, "I am starting to understand. The world leaders need not be ideologs and not be deceiving their true loyalties. They must be truthful and be genuine to the ones they serve. Our leaders should advocate for their respective nations. Besides, if your national leaders do not speak for their respective countries, who will?"

Aristides responded, "Yes, I think that you are getting it!"

Solon responded, "Dad, thanks for this beneficial explanation! I have many questions; however, I think I need to get some rest. We can discuss this later and how to stop this insanity and make recommendations about what to do."

Aristides expressed, "Yes, we shall discuss more. You are correct that you need your rest. Aphrodite, please turn on AI Thirteen."

Aristides instructed Solon and AI Thirteen like he had the night before. "The instructions are the same as yesterday. We shall return at approximately seven a.m. tomorrow. AI Thirteen, do not disturb Solon until six a.m. AI Thirteen, please ensure that Solon has at least three days of nutritional substances consumed by the time we arrive. Like today, you may give one or two more days, if Solon requests more. AI Thirteen, there is one additional request. Please inform me of any unusual activity from Solon when he is sleeping, such as nervous twitches or talking in his sleep. By the way, tomorrow will be a long day again.

"Well, both of you have a good night's sleep. See you tomorrow."

AI Thirteen replied, "Sir, you have a good evening as well. I promise that I shall take good care of Solon."

They left the office. They took the same route they took the night before. As they were walking home, they saw the same laborer on the same sidewalk that they saw last night, as well as the night before. The laborer smiled, and she was happy to see them. The laborer made genuine eye contact and smiled.

The laborer thought to herself, *Great! I am fortunate to have a guardian that does not put the fear of hell in me.* She said respectfully, "Sir guardian and AI specialist, good evening, and I hope that you had a wonderful day!"

Aristides said pleasantly, "Good evening! Yes, we had a wonderful day in service to the STATE. Of course, thank you again for your devoted service to the GREAT STATE!"

The laborer smiled with delight and respect. She replied happily, "Thank you, honorable guardian! Have a wonderful evening as well! May the STATE bless you with honor and remembrance!"

5

DAYS 5 AND 6: PREPARATION DAYS

AS SOLON WAS RESTING IN HIS BED, he pondered, *Yesterday I discovered that I have two biological parents who seem to care for me and love me. I prefer to be cautious since I lack the experience to truly assess my thoughts and the situation. My limited awareness seems to indicate optimism for my parents' assistance and love. In addition, the good news is that AI Thirteen has been polite toward me lately. Mom has clearly reprogrammed him. I wonder what else has changed about AI Thirteen?*

AI Thirteen came to awaken Solon again. They did all the typical morning routines; however, there was one unusual item on the table. There was a flower next to Solon's protein drinks. Solon laughed and realized that he had one more piece of evidence.

Solon reflected, **Mom and Dad, you are both wonderful and remarkable! I wonder what other surprises await me.** AI Thirteen and Solon left for the medical office.

At their domicile, Solon's parents were sitting for breakfast. Aristides prayed aloud, *"As revealed in John 3:16–17: 'For God so loved the world, that he gave his only begotten Son, that whosoever believeth in him should not perish, but have everlasting life. For God sent not his Son into the world; but that the world through him might be saved.'*

"Lord, thank You for all Your blessings and for giving us Your son and sacrificing him for our sins. Grant us the skills and love to prepare Solon for his tests tomorrow, as well as to serve You for Your will and glory. Amen."

They finished their breakfast and left for the medical office. When they arrived, Aphrodite shut off AI Thirteen again. Aristides informed, "Solon, tomorrow will be your simulation test and another physical test. Be aware that the physical test has the three events that you did a couple of days ago. Expect the following three events: the first event, you need to run eight miles under sixty-six minutes and six seconds; the second event, you need to do three punches with each hand with an average 666 psi or over for both hands; and for the third event, there are three lifts with the highest being 666 pounds or higher. I am not concerned about these three events. I believe that you will pass all three with ease. Your mother will give you a powerful stimulant that will be activated when you wake up tomorrow.

"The major effort and focus must be to prepare you for the simulation test. You will be a team leader with four AI soldiers. The object is to terminate the Enemy Team Leader who also has four AI soldiers. Your AI soldiers may be sacrificed. Eliminating the enemy AI soldiers does not win the simulation. The enemy AI soldiers will surrender once the Enemy Team Leader is terminated. The Enemy Team Leader will not surrender regardless of the severity of its damage or overwhelming odds. No matter what, you must terminate and neutralize the Enemy Team Leader. In reality, the Team Leader is another AI robot who looks like an AE HUMAN. All weapons on both sides can kill or harm you. You should show no mercy. Their tactics will be basic. One last rule to remember is that the simulation test will end in sixteen minutes. If you are not dead or seriously injured and did not kill the enemy Team Leader, you will become an enlisted soldier. The commander, who will watch you, has the option of making you a sergeant. If you succeed and kill the enemy team leader without suffering serious injuries, then the commander could commission you as either a first or second lieutenant. You will then be given three days to learn your specialty, and then you will report to your assigned commander.

"We will start practicing by firing a simulated weapon. Please go to the rifle simulator, which is in the next room. There is no real ammo in this one; however, it acts and feels like an actual weapon that you will be issued tomorrow. Please recall and imagine the proper firing of an assault rifle. Next, you need to fire five shots at the target." Solon struggled with his technique and missed the target four times, with one just inside the outer ring.

Aristides expressed, "Relax! We need you to breathe properly. When you pull the trigger, you should not know when the rifle fires. In addition, you must hold your breath until the weapon fires. If you do not hold your breath, you will most likely miss the target." Solon shot the weapon several more times until he mastered it. Aristides changed the target to look like the enemy Team Leader. Solon continued to fire numerous times until he was shooting like an expert.

Solon pondered, *I am truly enjoying and savoring this! I believe that I have found my true calling! I love shooting these weapons! I cannot wait to terminate the enemy!*

Aristides proclaimed, "Good job! Next, you shall now learn how to low crawl. Recall and imagine a proper low crawl. Remember to remain low, as well as learn to low crawl quickly and quietly."

Solon practiced many times until he grasped it completely. Subsequently, Solon did the same thing with several other physical activities, from jumping to climbing. Aristides wanted to ensure that his muscle memory was first rate and that he was well trained.

Later, Aristides had Solon acquire the skills of handling an army knife. Furthermore, he ensured that Solon grasped and perfected several martial arts skills and moves. Aristides went over several military tactics and strategies to guarantee that Solon could easily defeat the enemy. Aristides knew that the first simulation test was for beginners and was easy to defeat; however, he was not willing to take any chances. Moreover, Aristides enjoyed and relished the time working diligently with his son.

Solon reflected while he was performing martial arts, *I am so fortunate to have my father. The time is obviously too short; however, at least I have parents compared to others. He appears to be taking the extra step to safeguard that I succeed and survive.*

In addition, I am highly motivated to have three more days with my parents; equally, I am despising and abhor the supposed GREAT STATE for depriving humans of their parents, families, as well as their childhood.

When training with the army knife and shooting the assault rifle, I felt alive with vitality. I felt I was born to be a soldier and found my true purpose and calling!

After a long morning and afternoon, they sat for their first meal together. Aphrodite prepared an excellent dinner since this would be Solon's first time eating genuine and solid food. Since Solon had his test the next day, he was authorized a steak and potatoes meal that was enough for all three of them. Aristides had some contraband soda, which the investigator gave him. In addition, Aristides got some genuine contraband portabella mushrooms and Caesar salad. These were examples of how Aristides had secretly developed ways to survive this cold world. Aristides, over time, had developed a trusted secretive network with others to obtain unauthorized items, since he was an enhancer. He took care of others by providing them with desperately needed medical services or drugs that were not approved. Everyone in the STATE realized when to be silent when someone took care of them. Ironically, he even took care of a powerful ELITE named ELITE Heraclitus.

They all sat at the table and prepared to eat. Aristides articulated joyfully, "Family, which has a magnificent ring to it, let us say grace.

"Lord, please keep Solon in the palm of Your Hands and prepare Solon for Your glory to do Your Will. He will be in harm's way tomorrow, which we do not fear since he is in Your hands. Please give mercy and comfort to all in this sinful world, even the godless ELITE. May we all find Your love and glorious purpose? As it is revealed in Psalm 23: 'Yea, though I walk through the shadow of death, I fear no evil: for thou art with me; thy rod and thy staff, they comfort me.' Amen."

Solon prayed aloud, *"God, thank You for giving me a family that loves me and cares for me. Amen."*

Solon struggled to eat his first meal; however, Aphrodite taught him how to eat properly without embarrassing him. After a few mistakes, Solon enjoyed his meal. His parents were pleased that Solon had no difficulty in keeping his food down. His body did not reject the food; however, Solon was famished, so Aphrodite prepared some protein drinks for him, as well.

Solon expressed, "I am so happy that I have you both in my life. I understand we need to keep our family and relationships concealed. I promise to Almighty God that I will keep this a secret among us, as well as our belief in the Almighty God.

"Mom, the dinner was sumptuous! I can honestly say that this meal was the best steak and potatoes that I have ever eaten. I am clearly looking forward to our next family meal."

Aphrodite responded, "That was hilarious! You have my sarcastic sense of humor. That is wonderful!"

They continued to have several delightful and meaningful family conversations. Although their relationship was deprived of a sufficient number of years to be a truly loving family with numerous common experiences, they were clearly bonding into a respectable and connected relationship. After an hour, Aphrodite and Aristides prepared to leave. Aphrodite went to AI Thirteen and activated him again and gave him the usual instructions. They said their goodbyes and headed to their respective domiciles for the night.

Aphrodite and Aristides were greeted by the laborer again, which was becoming routine. They were always concerned when walking home. Of course, there were security cameras and monitoring devices everywhere. Aphrodite had to be on her extreme best behavior since she did not desire that her true AE HUMAN identity be discovered. As Aphrodite behaved in a robotic manner, Aristides vigilantly checked for danger, as well as for vanguards or ELITES. The stroll was never a pleasant one. Their city, called **Utopianapolis,** was dreadfully gloomy, with no art, nature, or beauty. The only positive was that there was little concern from criminals or vandals. No one dared to violate the law or any governmental curfews; however, the heavy Orwellian boot of the tyrannical STATE protected absolute fear and ensured it was maintained.

Just before they arrived at their domicile, ELITE Seth approached them. They immediately stepped out of his way. Aristides expressed, "**HAIL TO THE GREAT STATE!** Sir, good evening! It is an honor to be in your glorious presence."

The ELITE Seth looked them over several times. His well-armed, daunting, oppressive guards moved into a clearly offensive position for ELITE Seth's protection. He seemed to examine them with great curiosity and scrutiny.

ELITE Seth proclaimed, "You are guardian enhancer Aristides. I believe that I shall evaluate a soldier that is currently under your care. Tomorrow, this soldier will be tested to be an officer. Is this true?" ELITE Seth was one of three ruling ELITES of the Federal Republic EMPIRE. He was the Archon, which had the power of creating laws. He did not respect the other two ruling ELITES, which held the Polemarch and Basileus positions.

Aristides replied, "Sir, yes, you speak with clarity and accuracy. The soldier is ready for your evaluation and consideration."

ELITE Seth, who was wearing a necklace with an "S," avowed, "That is excellent! You better be accurate. I loathe when my precious time is wasted for a mere AE HUMAN. If you are wrong and he fails, you will pay the ultimate price; however, we desire and expect exceptional officers for the glorious war. I am looking forward to the evaluation, especially the simulation. I enjoy a good deadly competition.

"Leave my sight and carry on! Guards, let them pass!"

Aristides humbly replied, "**HAIL TO THE GREAT STATE!** Sir, thank you and goodnight!"

As ELITE Seth and his devoted guards were departing, ELITE Seth pondered, *The encounter with the enhancer reminds me that we are heading in the right satanic direction. I have no respect for humanity because they have faith and trust in an absent god and in demanding religions. Moreover, this misguided faith in God has led to creating alleged fair and just laws. These laws protected the weak and useless, like the disabled, ailing, and decrepit. They need to evolve into a greater specie and humanity must go as the dodo bird. The enhancer, at least, assists in this end by performing artificial enhancements. I know that we must continue to transform to be supernatural-like in status and be godlike; of course, we must still revere Satan.*

Too many delusional and foolish atheist elites, like ELITE Heraclitus, respect many qualities of humanity like art and beauty, as well as the occasional exceptional human. This has clearly divided the elites into two rival camps. Furthermore, the atheist elites do not recognize any god, which includes the one veritable god, Satan. They do not understand that Satan did not abandon man and place unrealistic expectations, such as avoiding a sinful life. Religion always expected individuals to deny their desires to enhance their nature.

My prayers and devotion to Satan have been answered with his materialistic, worldly blessings. He has ensured that I am a satanic ELITE and not a mere human or AE HUMAN. Most importantly, I need not adhere to the empire's laws. I am the law."

Aristides and Aphrodite quickly left their sight. When they arrived at their residence, they immediately embraced and thanked the Lord for still being alive. She cried and showed her true human emotions.

She expressed, "Aristides, thank God, you did it again. Thank you for staying calm and responding correctly to that heartless evil ELITE. If his time is perceived to be squandered, he will kill you! I do not want to lose you or Solon!

"I do not know what I will do if I am ever interrogated or questioned! Nervously, I am afraid that we shall be caught because of my uncontrollable emotions! I love you! I am a total wreck now!" Aristides said nothing. He comforted and reassured her with his actions and love.

Early in the morning of the next day, Solon was reviewing in his mind the three exercises and military skills that he went over yesterday. He was amazed by the cornucopia of skills that he learned in such a short amount of time. Furthermore, he realized that his father was correct, that he must perform physical activities to acquire muscle memory. He felt self-confident and prepared for the simulation test.

At 7:00 a.m., they all arrived at the office. Aristides informed and reminded Solon of what he needed to know for today's tests. Aphrodite turned off AI Thirteen.

Aristides expressed, "Solon and I will go to the simulation test site. Aphrodite, if you wish, you may watch the event on my computer. Love, after Solon succeeds, laborers will bring over a celebratory meal for us. We will then have three days to prepare Solon for his first unit. Well, we are leaving. Take care, love."

She replied, "I love you both! God bless and Godspeed!"

They arrived at the simulation test site. They both went to

the area where Solon was required to register. Moreover, they were greeted by the same Test Proctor that tested Solon a couple of days ago.

The Test Proctor Guardian Titan proclaimed, "XY777-316-Q17-0001, with the STATE-approved named of Solon, is registered to take three physical tests. The identification number XY777-316-Q17-0001 will be confirmed in the system once you complete your officer specialty.

"If you pass the three physical events, then you will perform a combat simulation test as a Team Leader for a maximum of sixteen minutes. I will go over additional rules once you complete and pass the three physical tests. If you fail any one of the three physical tests, then you will become an enlisted soldier and will immediately report to your commander. Follow me to the exercise room."

Aristides reassured, "Solon, you have this!"

After approximately two hours, Solon and the Test Proctor Guardian returned. The Test Proctor informed, "Enhancer guardian, Solon has successfully completed and passed the three events.

"Solon's punch average was 1,400 psi for right hand and 1,580 psi for the left hand. He lifted an average of 1,200 pounds. Both events exceeded the 666 psi or 666 pounds minimum. Furthermore, his eight-mile run was under the sixty-six minutes and six seconds maximum time. His run time was thirty-eight minutes and eight seconds. Great job! Solon passed. Solon, you will have two hours to rest and eat. As is customary, you are rewarded an excellent STATE-approved meal of your choice since you are performing a combat mission or simulation test. Enjoy your meal and HAIL TO THE GREAT STATE!"

Aristides and Solon responded in kind and headed to the dining room. There were other soldiers there who were being tested or were part of the staff. After acquiring their meal, a captain requested to sit with them and the enhancer agreed and welcomed him.

The captain expressed, "I believe your name is Solon. If this is true, then if you complete and survive the test without killing the enemy, then you will be one of my sergeants. I saw the results for the three physical tests. You did exceptionally well! I wish the best for you."

Solon replied, "Sir, yes, I am Solon. Thank you for the compliment."

The captain expressed, "I'd like for you to be a sergeant in my command; however, I believe you would make an excellent officer. I hope that you succeed in passing the simulation test and are rewarded three additional days to earn your officer's specialty. Undoubtedly, you will become an officer and will be placed in a different command.

"By the way, I have completed two years of combat and numerous campaigns. My best advice that I can give you is to learn from the soldiers and officers that have survived combat for over three months. When you become an officer, listen to your seasoned sergeants and find a comrade or two to console with. Remember that we are all on the same team. Well, I shall leave you to enjoy your meal. Enhancer guardian, thank you for allowing me the pleasure of conversing with this honorable soldier. HAIL TO THE GREAT STATE!"

Solon replied, "Yes, sir! Thank you for your excellent advice! HAIL TO THE GREAT STATE!"

Aristides and Solon continued to eat. They both picked rib-eye steak and buttered lobster with a side Greek salad and loaded potato. Solon knew that this was the best meal ever; however, he would rather eat with both his parents. They realized they could not converse with each other while they were in the dining hall.

After the two hours and obtaining his gear and weapons from the quartermaster, Solon reported to Test Proctor Titan. Aristides went to the monitoring room where he could watch the simulation test. The test proctor assigned the four AI soldiers to Solon, which were conveniently numbered. The simulation room had several white shaped objects in it. Next, the test instructor turned on the simulation room, which transformed from the immense room into a lush jungle environment.

The Test Proctor Guardian Titan instructed, "Solon, the object is to terminate the enemy Team Leader who has four enemy AI soldiers. Once you terminate the Enemy Team Leader, the Enemy AI soldiers will surrender and the simulation ends. Both forces have the same weapons, which are assault rifles and knives, as well as the same amount of ammunition. You have sixty-six rounds. If you acquire an AI soldier or Team Leader's ammo or weapon, you may use them. Be informed that your helmet has the capability to send commands to your AI soldiers. In addition, there is a monitor in your helmet that allows you to see what your four AI soldiers visualize.

"You or your AI soldiers may not leave the simulation event during the live exercise. You will be executed if you or your AI soldiers do so.

"As a piece of advice, make sure that you terminate the Enemy Team Leader and not merely wound him. The enemy Team Leader will not quit. He will try to kill you to the end.

"This exercise has a maximum of sixteen minutes. If you are still alive and not seriously injured and have not terminated the enemy Team Leader, you will be promoted to sergeant and will report to your new commander tomorrow. If you succeed in the mission, you will be promoted to second lieutenant. I shall give you additional information after the exercise. Guards, begin the timer. Solon, the exercise has started. May you have STATE speed!"

Solon analyzed the terrain and his surroundings. Solon could hear two enemy AI scouts who were probably a hundred meters away. He commanded two AI soldiers to start in the opposite direction of the two enemy AI scouts. He commanded the third and fourth AI soldiers to remain and take cover. Solon began to low crawl toward the two enemy AI scouts. They were separated by about thirty meters. He reached the first one with no detection. He took his knife quietly from his sheath. He stealthily surprised the enemy AI soldier from the rear and he cut off his head. The other AI enemy scout came in his direction. He noticed that this enemy AI scout did not detect him. He remained silent, and he allowed the AI enemy scout to pass him by without detection. Next, he activated the visual screen in his helmet. Fortunately, the two AI soldiers that he had sent in the opposite direction had visual contact with the enemy Team Leader. He commanded them to take aim and remain concealed. He commanded them to await his command to fire. Solon started to low crawl to a tree that was in the rear of the enemy team leader. Solon was approximately ten meters away from his desired target. He had a clean shot to the back of the head of the Enemy Team Leader. He placed his assault rifle on automatic and blew the Enemy Team Leader's head off and then blew a hole in his back, as well. Then, immediately, the remaining enemy AI soldiers raised their hands to surrender. The simulation finished, and the room went to pure white, with all the AI soldiers either terminated or inactivated.

The Test Proctor Guardian pondered to himself, *Fantastic! Another enemy prisoner is executed and Solon believes that he terminated an AI robot instead of killing a convicted AE HUMAN. The ELITE will be pleased and I will be awarded again. These prisoners do not deserve to live since they rebelled against the great STATE. They do not appreciate all that the STATE does for them. All citizens should appreciate how secure their lives are without the concerns of chaotic, unpredictable society. I like the fact that our lives are completely orderly and predictable.*

The Test Proctor Guardian Titan stated from a loudspeaker, "That is excellent! You completed the simulation in less than six minutes! Head toward my voice and I shall tell you what will happen next. Guardian enhancer, meet us at my location.

"Solon, since you passed the simulation test and completed the mission, you are now promoted to second lieutenant. Furthermore, you are given three more days to complete your officer's specialty. You have earned your first medal, which will be awarded to you after you have completed your officer course. You will continue to be under the care of the guardian enhancer. Furthermore, once I release you, report to the quartermaster for your first issue and turn in your weapons and gear.

"As an additional opportunity, if you elect, there is a test called the Gladiator Challenge that the GREAT STATE is offering. This challenge would occur after completing and passing your officer specialty test. This glorious and excellent opportunity is to participate in a gladiator event against captured enemy AI robotic soldiers, which is televised for all to see, which, of course, includes the all-knowing ELITES. If you succeed and pass this test, then you will be given three additional days with the enhancer for rest and relaxation, as well as be promoted to first lieutenant. I think that the GREAT STATE, as always, has developed another outstanding program! Solon, congratulations again! You and the enhancer are dismissed! HAIL TO THE GREAT STATE!"

Solon and Aristides responded appropriately and headed to the quartermaster area. Solon was issued two blue dress officer uniforms and three green combat uniforms. He was issued an officer's sword, which he was authorized to wear with his blue dress uniform. Next, the quartermaster issued him the same army knife Solon carried and used during the simulation test. The sword and knife had his number and name emgraved into them. The army knife could be worn with both uniforms. He could not have a firearm for casual wear. Firearms were only issued for soldiers and officers in approved combat zones; however, field-grade officers, major or higher, could carry weapons at all times.

Next, a vanguard swore him in as an officer and congratulated him. The vanguard remarked that Solon did an exceptional strategic attack against the enemy team leader's forces. He encouraged him to take up the Gladiator Challenge and stated that Solon would be a superior first lieutenant. The vanguard dismissed them. Solon went and dressed in his blue dress uniform and placed his other uniforms and clothing in his duffel bag.

They headed to Aristides's office, which was not too far away. After about a mile, they took a turn down a gloomy, dark alley, which was basically a shortcut. Unfortunately, Aristides saw two dead guards, and an ELITE surrounded by two perceived villains. Solon immediately pulled out his knife and one villain attacked him. Solon side kicked the villain in the stomach, which resulted in the villain slamming into the alley wall. The other villain attempted to outflank him; however, Solon drew his sword and mightily swung it. This resulted in the villain's head being removed. The villain dropped dead. The other villain attempted to get up; however, Solon immediately decapitated him. As this was all occurring, Aristides was medically attending to the ELITE.

The ELITE Heraclitus, who was wearing an "A" necklace, expressed with gratitude, "That was an excellent performance and service to the glorious STATE! You are Solon, the one that won at the simulation test today! Two great engagements in one day! That is outstanding! Solon, you shall be awarded and recognized for this. However, you are both ordered to be silent of this incidence, but your silence shall be significantly awarded.

"Moreover, you both are ordered to be my guards until I relieve you! I need you both to protect me back to the simulation center. Enhancer, I believe, fortunately, that we have met previously. I believe that I am familiar with your outstanding work!" ELITE Heraclitus was one of three ELITES that ruled the Federal Republic EMPIRE. He was the Basileus ELITE, which was considered a ceremonial position and occasionally a tie breaker of the other two ELITES. He was allied with the ELITE Mars. Both of these ELITES were despised by ELITE Seth.

Aristides replied, "Yes, we did. It was a few months ago for another soldier's test evaluation. By the way, do you have any injuries? I have a few medical supplies."

ELITE Heraclitus was appreciative that Aristides did not mention medically treating him on several occasions. Aristides had, on numerous occasions, issued him unauthorized medicine and performed unauthorized medical assistance. ELITE Heraclitus understood that he could never show weakness or vulnerability; if he did, many vanguards or elites would pounce on the opportunity. ELITE Heraclitus had a rare disease that he clearly did not want anyone to know about. The ELITE Heraclitus expressed, "No, nothing serious. If you have a painkiller, I will be deeply appreciative."

Aristides gave him a couple of highly effective painkillers, and they headed back to the simulation building. After a quarter of a mile, five additional guards came up.

The ELITE Heraclitus declared, "You both did outstanding! Solon, you shall take the Gladiator Challenge, and I am confident that you shall be victorious. As I stated, Solon, you will be rewarded and recognized for your heroism. However, you both shall say nothing of this.

"Guards, make sure that they have special rations sent to them for the next three days. Lieutenant Solon and guardian enhancer, you are dismissed! You are both vital assets to the GREAT STATE! Lieutenant Solon, I will monitor your expected great military service! I will see you in three days! HAIL TO THE GREAT STATE!"

They replied in kind and immediately headed toward Aristides's office. They remained silent for the entire walk.

Solon thought to himself, *I do not know what to think. I am extremely appreciative that my parents have properly prepared me to excel in tactical and martial skills. However, I have not been prepared to take the life of other AE HUMANS, even if they are villains. I feel that I may have done something wrong. I need my parents' insight and wisdom.*

Aristides pondered intensely, *Thank God that we are still alive! I do not know if saving the life of the ELITE was the right decision. However, Solon does not have the life experience to access the moral ramifications of choosing between the alleged villains and an ELITE. However, as I have experienced previously, ELITE Heraclitus seems to be appreciative and is well known for appreciating humans that he deemed to possess greatness and exceptional skills. I know that as long as I remain silent about ELITE Heraclitus's rare and unusual medical condition and prescribe him needed medicine, we shall be fine.*

As they arrived at the office door, two guards presented the promised rations. The guards left immediately after congratulating Solon again, as well as reminding him that he had witnessed nothing. However, this would be on his top-secret record, which would be only seen by ELITES and vanguards.

Aphrodite came from the back room; she had a terrified expression on her face. Aphrodite stated, "Oh, thank God! I thought something terrible had happened to both of you since you took so long to get home! Prior to the additional rations, a couple of laborers came by with our special dinner for Solon becoming an officer."

Aristides replied, "Let us eat and we will tell you what happened." After they said grace, they all sat down to the remarkable delivered prepared meal, which included roast beef, mashed potatoes with brown gravy, and plenty of bread and fruits. Aristides told Aphrodite what happened. Aphrodite was extremely proud of Solon; however, she expressed her concern and distrust of any ELITE. Aristides expressed his concurrence with her. Aphrodite mentioned that the simulation test was not available on the internet; so she continued to improve AI Thirteen's program and prepared for Solon's officer specialty training that would be needed for the next three days. Aristides recommended that Solon come with them and stay at their domicile that night. Solon was delighted with the idea. AI Thirteen remained inactivated and stayed in his office. After cleaning the area, they left and headed to their domicile.

6.

NEXT THREE DAYS: GLADIATOR CHALLENGE

WHILE WATCHING THE TELEVISED STATE PROPAGANDA, Aphrodite was fixing an exceptional breakfast for her family. She was filled with genuine enthusiasm and elation about having her loving family together. She felt truly alive and thankful to God for all her gifts.

Unfortunately, the STATE media was televising and advertising how great the ELITE and empire were. The fake, dishonest media advertised and marketed how great the "glorious" war effort was flourishing. The media emphasized how the empire was winning the glorious war. Moreover, the disgraceful media reminded everyone that they must perform their part and service for the GREAT STATE, and to receive their monthly vaccine shots.

As the media was spewing its tautological propaganda, Solon came and was ready for another long, challenging day. He hugged his mom and articulated, "I am sorry that you are worried about us. Thank you for your love and concern for us."

Aristides walked in and smiled. He spoke. "Solon, I hope you slept well on the sofa."

Solon expressed, "Yes, I did. Thank you, Dad. Do we have time to talk?"

Aristides responded, "Yes, what do you desire to discuss?"

Solon stated, "I have been only conscious for six days now and probably only possess language for the same amount of time. I possess no memories or experiences prior to my initial awakening.

Furthermore, AI Thirteen stated that the initial developmental period took 1,666 days. You stated that I needed to develop muscle memory, and I concur, and this advice has been significantly beneficial; however, from my current experiences and activities, I was not required to develop muscle memory for ambulatory activities like walking and arising from a seated position or bending my arms or legs or numerous other activities. This makes little sense to me. Please explain why."

Aristides expressed, "I am impressed with your inquisitiveness and your desire to seek the truth. The short answer is that your so-called initial awakening was not your true initial wakening. To explain the entire process, you were conceived in an artificial womb with your parent's egg and sperm. Next, after a couple months, you were placed in an adjustable incubator, which expands as the AE HUMAN grows.

"You were awakened regularly, generally weekly, to be monitored and tested, as well as to assist in your proper development. Furthermore, your initial chip with your language software and other initial software was installed in your back. This occurred a week before your initial awakening. Thus, you probably had dreams and thoughts with language a day or two before your initial awakening. In addition, these chips and upgraded memory device subpress any memories prior to the initial awakening.

"Unfortunately, once you were transferred to your artificial incubator, the weekly awakening was primarily used to test and determine if you could continue to exist since we are just all STATE property and we are considered expendable. By the grace of God, your parents were assisting you in your development, which included teaching you to crawl and walk, as well as drink and chew your food properly. On a positive note, your mother truly enjoyed teaching you to crawl and walk. Furthermore, she played and held you regularly to safeguard your humanity and psychological development to be a success. The GREAT STATE forbids any cuddling or hugging of children; thanks to your loving mother, she violated the law and loved you regularly. I also played games with you and held you as well.

"For full disclosure, since the STATE is heartless and only tolerates a few genetic and biological imperfections, we protected you from having any noticeable defects. For example, you are left-handed, which does not score well; yet, we spent extra time to guarantee that you scored highly by becoming ambidextrous. However, you are still left-hand dominant, as well as left-foot dominant. For example, you still prefer to kick a ball with your left foot.

"Fortunately, administratively speaking, I was able to switch you with a baby that had died a couple days after conception; thus, I used that baby's assigned artificial womb for you. Prior to the baby's death, the baby clearly was within STATE standards; fortunately, the baby departed without the awareness of anyone."

Solon responded, "Thank you! That makes sense to me."

They finished getting ready and headed to the office. When they arrived, there was a well-wrapped package at the door for Solon. After settling, Solon opened the unique package and discovered a gift from the ELITE Heraclitus with a beautiful handwritten note. The gift was a silver and gold officer knife with Solon's name and identification number already engraved on it. This rarely awarded well-designed knife was for bravery and valor. The note read that ELITE Heraclitus congratulated Lieutenant Solon and looked forward to promoting him to first lieutenant and awarding him his medals. This was because he shall be victorious in the Gladiator Challenge. Furthermore, there was a military order that Second Lieutenant Solon must participate in the Gladiator Challenge on the day of graduation after completion of his Officer Specialty, which was expected to be completed in three days.

Aristides expressed, "Solon, congratulations! We now know what we need to concentrate on for the next two days. First, the Officer Specialty course will focus on Combat Engineering and basic staff officer skills. You already have the downloads. Thus, we shall only need to review the test format and how to avoid examination pitfalls. You need to achieve seventy percent of a one-hundred question multiple guess test. Therefore, our focus will primarily be on the Gladiator Challenge, which I presume is like the Gladiator Games that are partaken in March. The March Gladiator Games are a GLUE sponsored event for all the world, with the eight empires competing. Moreover, all wars cease temporarily in order to allow soldiers to participate in the games. The games are to entertain the EMPIRES' citizens and ELITES, as well as terminate war prisoners with supposed honor."

Aristides explained that if his assumptions were correct, Solon should be issued an army knife, sword, throwing knives and stars, and a pistol with one or two rounds; Solon should be authorized an armor vest and a helmet. Aristides expressed that the enemy, which might be three or four AI soldiers or humans, were each only equipped with a knife with no armor or a helmet. They proceeded to the other room and Solon used the simulator to practice the use of these weapons and tactics.

They entered the holographic and exercise room and Solon commenced to practice with the weapons. After Solon understood the basic tactics and usages of one of the weapons, then Solon could fight holographic enemy soldiers in mock scenarios to confirm mastery of said weapon. Aristides monitored his progress and gave excellent practical and succinct advice regularly. He was confident that Solon would succeed; however, he was not willing to gamble with Solon's life. Their dedication resulted in basically missing lunch. Aphrodite came in to check on them. She placed sandwiches and drinks on a table for them when they took an abrupt break. They both just devoured the food and drinks when Solon required rest between activities.

Aristides advised, "Remember what Sun Tzu emphasized. You must know yourself and your enemy. Study your surroundings and do not underestimate your enemy."

At approximately 2000 hours, Aphrodite interrupted them and insisted that they depart for home in order to eat dinner and rest.

As they were strolling home, Solon pondered to himself, *Well, I am extremely pleased with knowing that my parents oversaw my development for my first 1,666 days. This seems to have secured my humanity and improved my development.*

I do not know what to think about the ELITES' gift and being ordered to the Gladiator Challenge. At least my father has formulated a thoughtful plan to succeed in this next challenge. Moreover, my mother expressed her concern and love toward us. My parents have been a true Godsend.

I am believing that many societal and governmental decisions by the ELITES and others were made without considering our humanity. It is a utopia for the ELITE, not for the people.

Before they left, there were additional unexpected rations for them, which they delightfully took with them. When they arrived at their domicile, there was an ELITE Guard waiting for them with a gift-wrapped box and another note. The Guard stated, "The ELITE Heraclitus has sent you this fine vintage wine with imported cheese. Honorable ELITE Heraclitus sends his sincere invitation for guardian enhancer Aristides to attend Second Lieutenant Solon's award ceremony and his Gladiator Challenge. He also expressed his deepest thanks for what you have sworn confidentiality and secrecy to. He expressed that it is his sincere belief that Solon is advancing toward greatness and military glory." After the Guard expressed some kind words and congratulations, he departed.

Aristides spoke, "Well, that was a pleasant surprise! Love, we have never imbibed wine together, especially a fine vintage red wine! What rations were issued?"

Aphrodite showed them that they would have lobsters, shrimp, and potatoes with other mixed vegetables. She immediately commenced to preparing the fine meal. She could not wait to imbibe the fine wine; so she immediately poured a few glasses.

After Aphrodite secured the area, she joked, "Solon, I think that you and I are not old enough to drink. Well, your father is the only one who has been on this earth for at least twenty-one years; however, he does not look it. I guess, given all our treasonous acts and capital offenses, this is just a minor violation and misdemeanor. They can only execute us once! Besides, we may now have an ELITE on our side!"

While Aphrodite was preparing the exceptional meal, Solon stated, "Dad, thanks for teaching me today! I deeply appreciate it. May we continue our conversation on how the world got to this tyrannical state? You finished your last point with the countries throughout the world gradually becoming tyrannical surveillance states for the globalist."

Aristides replied, "Yes, I shall. Russia was still at war with the Ukraine. Many countries depended on Russian oil. One such country, Germany, was completely dependent on Russian oil and was cut off since Russia was still at war. The German government and alleged president were committed to the unreliable net zero energy agenda. This resulted in numerous deaths from freezing during the next few harsh winters. Furthermore, numerous other countries suffered the same dismal fate. Over one billion people lost their lives, which was over one eighth of the world's population."

Aristides reiterated that the Netherlands required its farmers to reduce the use of fertilizer; this resulted in the Netherlands no longer having excess food for other countries. He emphasized that even in the United States, their farmers were required to reduce the use of fertilizer. This resulted in additional starvation throughout the world, especially in third world countries. This led to an additional two billion lives lost, as well as civil unrest and the collapse of numerous governments. The widespread famine led to disease and civil wars, as well as massive migration. Aristides stressed that governments declared martial law and became police states practically overnight. The Orwellian nightmare was in full swing.

Solon asked, "Who was the last holdout?"

He replied, "The United States' Constitution, which was the last holdout for the world, was under relentless attack. Since the United States' southern border was undefended and completely vulnerable, migrants and illegals crossed at will. The unrestricted migration increased exponentially since people were desperately seeking employment and food, as well as a better life for their families, since their governments were collapsing. In addition, the United States' political demographics were altering from the illegal migrations. The Marxist elements of the country succeeded in packing the supreme court, which eventually corroded the constitutional rights of its citizenry. In addition, the changing political landscape led to the United States removing its right to bear arms and freedom of speech. The tyrannical globalist goal was nearly complete!"

Solon asked, "What else was going on at the same time?"

He answered, "During the same time, the globalist banks did a great reset and created global electronic money with no currency. All transactions were under the control of the global ELITES."

Aristides explained that in order to have credits and employment, you needed to submit to injecting a chip in your hand to guarantee complete monitoring and paying for services and goods. Moreover, executive orders digitized the United States' currency, which eliminated paper money and allowed the deep state to monitor all economic transactions, as well as punish people for not complying with refusing to use the digital currency or purchasing unauthorized items like ammunition. The control was complete. He stressed that the globalists had economic control over all purchases by an individual, as well as their lives.

Aristides stated, "Trans-humanism was their next diabolical end! Global companies like PERFECT-BABY were created that took over pregnancy and early infant development. Parents, at first, were willing to do this since they could order their supposed ideal baby from the color of their eyes to their cognitive abilities to athletic abilities. Of course, the ELITES took this over as well and determined the selection process.

"Solon, please let us discuss this more later. Your mother has prepared dinner, and it looks delicious."

Solon responded, "Yes, I am famished!"

Aphrodite stated, "Dinner is ready. Solon, please say grace."

Solon prayed aloud, *"Lord, thank You for my loving parents and for allowing me to have this time with them.*

"As revealed in 1 Corinthians 13:4–8, Charity suffereth long, and is kind; charity envieth not; charity vaunteth not itself, is not puffed up, Doth not behave itself unseemly, seeketh not her own, is not easily provoked, thinketh no evil; Rejoiceth not in iniquity, but rejoiceth in the truth; Beareth all things, believeth all things, hopeth all things, endureth all things. Charity never faileth: but whether there be prophecies, they shall fail; whether there be tongues, they shall cease; whether there be knowledge, it shall vanish away."

They enjoyed the fine wine and the delicious meal. They had several wonderful conversations and togetherness for the next several hours.

Aphrodite stated, "I do not desire to ruin this delightful evening by stating something that I strongly desire to occur but may only be an unfulfilled dream.

"Aristides, I love you with all my heart and soul, and I know you feel the same way. I know that we have said our vows to each other, but I'd love for us to be married by a reverend or priest. My heart feels that I am only your paramour. My head knows differently, and I always want to be your lover. The wine is probably talking, making me reveal my desires and dreams."

Aristides responded, "Love, I feel the same way, but—"

Solon interrupted and expressed, "Mom and Dad, I have

a potential solution! Tomorrow, please download the STATE-forbidden and outlawed chaplain specialty into me. Then, tomorrow evening, I will marry you both as an ordained chaplain!"

Aphrodite responded, "That is a wonderful and beautiful idea! That is a brilliant family gift that I would always cherish!"

Aristides responded, "Son, great idea! We shall make it happen. Your mother will be delighted that we fulfilled her dream.

"So, let us call it a splendid evening. Good night, Solon!"

Solon went to lie down on the sofa. He pondered, *I am extremely grateful that my training in the holograph and exercise room was beneficial. I believe that I am reasonably prepared for the Gladiator Challenge.*

Moreover, I feel practically prepared for the Combat Engineer Specialty test. When I had breaks today, I reviewed the material in my head. Matter of fact, I should review some of it before I go to sleep.

The next morning, they all prepared for a long and productive day. Without delay, they got ready. Once they arrived, Aphrodite went to check on AI Thirteen. Solon laid on the medical bed. Aristides prepared him to be downloaded with unauthorized chaplain specialty and other downloads. After an hour, the downloads were completed. Aristides had developed a sophisticated device within Solon that could hide unauthorized files or downloads. Basically, when the STATE scanned Solon, they read what was authorized.

Next, Aristides and Solon sat down at Aristides's desk. He instructed Solon about the Combat Engineer Specialty test.

Aristides tutored Solon on several pitfalls of the test. He emphasized to read all the answers and pick the best answer. Furthermore, he reminded him that there would be plenty of time to take the test. There were one hundred questions, and he would have three hours to take the test. Aristides made sure that Solon reviewed the required information. Aristides ensured he experienced every potential type of problem at least twice.

After a few hours of preparing for the Combat Engineer Specialty test, they returned to the holograph and exercise room. Solon reviewed everything that he did yesterday. He truly was mastering the weapon skills and military tactics and strategies. He was becoming a true guru of the sword and the knife.

At around 5:00 p.m., Aphrodite entered the room. She insisted that they should proceed to their home since Solon needed to get a good night's sleep for tomorrow's events.

When they arrived at their domicile, Solon requested, "Mom and Dad, let us prepare for your wedding. I shall wear my dress uniform and be your minister."

Aphrodite changed into white labor clothes that she had from an earlier time in her life. She looked radiant and stunning. She, of course, was holding a gorgeous flower. Aristides wore his gold guardian enhancer outfit. He looked distinguished and handsome.

In the living room, Lieutenant Solon, in his prominent blue officer's dress uniform with his officer sword, began the simple and delightful wedding. Solon said all the appropriate and eloquent words that ensured that his mother had a beautiful smile on her lovely face.

Solon ended with these ultimate words, ***"As revealed in Ephesians 5:28–30: 'So ought men to love their wives as their*** *own bodies. He that loveth his wife loveth himself. For no man ever yet hated his own flesh; but nourisheth and cherisheth it, even as the Lord the church: For we are members of his body, of his flesh, and of his bones.'*

"Mom and Dad, I pronounce you both as husband and wife. Dad, you may kiss the bride, who is my mom."

Solon hugged his parents and congratulated them both on their nuptial blessed union. They then ate an exceptional meal that Aphrodite prepared and finished the bottle of fine wine. Aphrodite expressed her deepest appreciation to her son for being their chaplain. They all called it an early evening, since Solon needed his rest.

The next day was the big day. They got ready quickly and headed to the office for some final preparation. After a couple hours of studying, Solon and Aristides headed to the simulation test site. They passed all the check points and scanners without detection of any unauthorized downloads or enhancements. Solon was saluted by a couple of soldiers when he entered the building. Then he saluted a superior officer as they headed down the corridor. He arrived at the registration room, and they were met by the same test proctor. After Solon completed his registration, Aristides headed to the monitoring room.

The Test Proctor Titan declared, "Second Lieutenant, I know that you have been very busy preparing, and I believe it will be a successful day for you! ELITE Heraclitus wishes you STATE-speed! Follow me to the exam room." In the room, there were other soldiers and officers taking tests in separate small cubicles.

The Test Proctor Titan instructed, "This test has one hundred multiple-choice questions. You have three hours to complete the test. You need a score of seventy to pass. I recommend you take your time and read each answer; however, do not spend too much time on a particular question. This test is pass or fail. If you fail, then you have three hours to look over the missed questions, and then you will take a similar test again. If you fail again, then you will no longer be an officer and you will become a staff sergeant. Good luck! You may proceed!"

After approximately two hours, Second Lieutenant Solon completed the test. His computer monitor flashed a score of eighty-eight.

The Test Proctor arrived, clearly delighted, and informed, "Lieutenant, congratulations! You passed, and you are branch qualified as a Combat Engineer, 'Q.' At 1500, which is approximately three hours from now, you need to report to the simulation room for the Gladiator Challenge. Meet the enhancer for lunch in the cafeteria. Next, you will need to proceed to see the quartermaster in order to be issued your weapons and equipment. I recommend that you take all that he issues to you for the challenge. I know you will succeed! Be aware that ELITE Heraclitus and other honorable guests will view this glorious event! Once you are triumphant, you will have your well-deserved reward and promotion ceremony. I shall give you additional instructions prior to the challenge. You are dismissed for lunch!"

After their excellent meal, they left for the quartermaster room. Solon was issued the weapons that he had practiced and mastered earlier. His pistol had only two rounds. Aristides departed for the monitor room. Lieutenant Solon left for the Gladiator Challenge registration room.

Test Proctor Titan instructed, "Lieutenant, welcome to this glorious event and, of course, congratulations on making it this far! I shall give you your instructions. First, the object is to terminate all three enemy AI soldiers. If you succeed, you shall be promoted to First Lieutenant and given a three-day pass. Second, you may quit or surrender; however, you will lose your commission and be demoted to the rank of staff sergeant. Third, if you are seriously injured, you will probably be gloriously terminated. Fourth, you are not authorized to show any mercy. Fifth, be aware that the wall around the colosseum is electrified with enough electricity to guarantee termination. Sixth, the event has a maximum time of thirty-six minutes. If you have not terminated all three AI enemies by this time, then the ELITES watching the event will determine your fate. Do you have any questions?"

Lieutenant Solon responded, "No! I am ready! HAIL TO THE GREAT STATE!" He entered into the spectacular colosseum, which was an extremely large open area. He estimated that it was slightly larger than three hundred meters. He could see all three AI enemies on the other side, and all of them were wearing different colors. There were many surveillance cameras on the ceilings; however, there were no spectators. However, Solon could hear fans yelling "victory" and "death to the enemy."

The three AI soldiers spread out. Solon ran toward the RED AI soldier, which was left of the other two. The RED AI soldier charged toward Solon. The BLUE AI soldier clearly stepped too close to the wall. Solon pulled out his pistol and shot the BLUE AI soldier in the chest. The damaged BLUE AI soldier smashed against the electrifying wall and was terminated immediately. This resulted in a spectacular sparkling electrical show that petrified and froze the other two AI soldiers. Over a loudspeaker, an announcer proclaimed, "One down and two to go! Let's go, GLADIATOR! Bring more glory to the GREAT STATE!"

Solon was still sprinting toward the RED AI soldier, who had stopped in a defensive position. Before he reached the RED AI soldier, Solon leaped in the air. He jumped over the RED AI soldier and turned in the air and landed behind him. Solon swiftly unsheathed his sword, and with one mighty swing, removed the RED AI soldier's arm that was holding its weapon. Then, he sliced off his other arm and then cut off his head. The announcer screamed, "That was a glorious death! Two down and one to go! Let's go, GLORIOUS GLADIATOR! Bring to the GREAT STATE another victory!" The GREEN AI had gained an additional knife, and now had one for each hand.

Solon and the GREEN AI slowly moved toward the center of the colosseum. Once Solon arrived at his desired point of attack, he honorably bowed to the GREEN AI soldier. The GREEN AI soldier did the same. The announcer stated, "We shall have a glorious death and fight! These warriors have demonstrated true honor toward each other! The ELITES and honored guests are witnessing an exceptional fight!"

Solon tossed his weapons to the side except for his knife, which he held in his right hand. The GREEN AI tossed one of his knives. Each warrior faced each other for nearly a minute, which felt like an eternity. You could have heard a pin drop during the eternal elapsed time.

They were only ten or twelve feet away from each other. GREEN AI soldier executed the first move and charged toward Solon. Solon blocked the knife swing with his right arm and then punched the AI in the head with his deadly left. That mighty and devastating punch knocked the AI soldier to the ground. The AI soldier strived to rise; however, Solon landed a powerful side kick in the AI soldier's stomach. Solon then stabbed the GREEN AI soldier in the neck, which was clearly a fatal blow. Lieutenant Solon bowed with respect toward his enemy. The announcer shouted excitedly, "The GLORIOUS GLADIATOR is victorious! What an exciting Gladiator Challenge! Let us chant, 'HAIL THE GREAT STATE!'" The announcer continued to entertain the ELITES and honored guests, as Solon stood victorious in the center of the grand colosseum. After a few minutes, instructions were given to Solon to attend his promotion and award ceremony.

The Test Proctor Titan pondered to himself, *Well, the lieutenant succeeded again! Three more dead enemy humans for the satanic ELITES' rituals and feasts! The satanic ELITES will be pleased!*

Solon pondered, *Why are the AI robots bleeding profusely like a human would? Furthermore, why am I able to see their internal organs and bones? This is very suspicious. It is possible that the STATE wants the deaths of AI robots to be realistic in order to entertain the audience. However, I felt that the blood and gore was similar to killing the villains.*

The ELITE Heraclitus announced, "I would like to begin by recognizing the ELITES and honored guests that watched this spectacular event! In addition, I would like to recognize the guardian enhancer Aristides for enhancing Solon to an exceptional warrior! They are both exceptional assets to the glorious STATE! First, we shall promote Second Lieutenant Solon to First Lieutenant Solon, which is truly well deserved."

The ceremony continued, and First Lieutenant Solon was awarded three medals, which were to be represented by three ribbons on his dress uniform. One was the third highest heroic medal that a soldier could receive for valor. The other two were merely for completing qualifications as a soldier and combat engineer specialty. Furthermore, he was bestowed the bronze gladiator badge, which was the lowest level of the three badges; however, the gladiator badges were rarely presented.

The ELITE Heraclitus informed, "First Lieutenant Solon, I have had the great honor of talking with your future commander. He requested that you be deployed to his unit ASAP, so you will be shipped out tomorrow at 2100 hours. I wish you further glory and STATE-SPEED."

Solon thought to himself, *I have been cheated out of my three-day pass. Well, it sounded too good to be true. It is obvious that what drives the STATE is the war effort!*

Aristides and Solon met with the quartermaster to turn in the weapons and equipment, as well as First Lieutenant Solon being issued a new dress uniform with appropriate ribbons and the badge on it. The quartermaster also gave him a device for his knife and sword to recognize his rank. The quartermaster was kind by allowing Solon to keep his original dress uniform.

They headed to their domicile. When they arrived, Aphrodite greeted them immediately, and she had a meal ready for them. Solon said nothing; however, he gave his original uniform to his mom. She cried immediately and embraced Solon and Aristides.

They heard the doorbell. Solon met a guard who delivered three bottles of vintage white wine from ELITE Heraclitus with a note. The note stated that the fine wine was for the three days of cancelled leave, and Heraclitus emphasized that Solon would be successful and they would meet again. ELITE Heraclitus also emphasized that he would be delighted to monitor his expected exceptional military service.

The guard departed, and they immediately opened one bottle of wine. They all three remained silent. After about an hour of drinking, Solon asked, "Since we are all intoxicated, Dad, please give me some philosophical and much-needed life advice."

Aristides pontificated and advised, *"Here is my advice to you, even when I am intoxicated.*

"Happiness should not be the only desired end. Happiness is temporal and fleeting, as well as confused by hedonistic ends. Remember one of Samurai Miyamoto Musashi's principles of Dokkōdō: 'Do not seek pleasure for its own sake.' Furthermore, love and duty are greater ends. As revealed in Mathew 22:37 with Jesus stating the greatest commandment: 'Thou shalt love the Lord thy God with all your heart, with all your soul, and with all thy mind.'"

Solon curiously stated, "What else would you advise?"

He responded, *"Well, always strive for meaning and purpose, as well as always speak and demonstrate the truth. As revealed in John 8:3: 'And you will know the truth, and the truth will set you free.' Furthermore, strive and become competent in needed skills for your chosen purpose and your chosen endeavors. Be responsible for your actions and choices. Strive toward your greatest purpose that has the highest responsibility and competency in your life that will yield the greatest good and fulfillment for oneself and humanity. Always give more for humanity and others than you will ever receive. Strive to be, as Marcus Aurelius expressed: 'Do your job, without whining.'"*

Solon interrupted, "Well, my purpose has been determined by the GREAT STATE. I shall be a soldier, but I do not know if this is my true calling. The STATE seems to be willing to sacrifice me for their ends, and I have no rights deemed by the STATE."

Aristides continued, *"Remember that God has made all humans as divine sovereign individuals. Human rights do not come from the government, they come from God. However, remember that rights come with great responsibility and upholding principles.*

"As Aristotle stated: 'Humans are rational animals.' However, we must remember to love and appreciate the arts, the beauty, and mythos, as well. They are poly-vocal and may speak with over one tongue without the limitation of a single language. Logic and rationality are not the complete end. As Confucius revealed: 'Everything has beauty, but not everyone sees it.'

"Furthermore, Aristotle also stated: 'We become just by the practice of just actions, self-controlled by exercising self-control, and courageous by performing acts of courage.' Strive to be Aristotelian sophron. In other words, determine the right judgement with the right actions.

"Appreciate the Buddhists' teaching that 'life is suffering' and the Christians' teaching 'to bear your cross.' However, I prefer to state it this way: 'life is a struggle,' since life has suffering and happiness, as well as its encouraging times and discouraging times; however, we all shall always struggle at all times, regardless. To struggle is part of our nature and must be accepted."

Solon stated, "I concur that life is a struggle. Since I am fortunate to have parents, unlike others, I am struggling with having parents because I fear losing you both."

His father responded, *"I have one more piece of advice. You should strive to be loving, sacrificial, and compassionate, as Jesus demonstrated; furthermore, strive to be stoic and wise as Marcus Aurelius ruled; moreover, strive to be as disciplined and focused as Samurai Miyamoto Musashi fulfilled. In addition, find beauty and wisdom in everything as Confucius experienced; furthermore, strive to have eudaimonia, live a virtuous life and be a sophron as Aristotle taught; and finally, strive to have the duty and devotion to philosophical commitment as the great philosophers and thinkers lived and revealed."*

Solon nodded with agreement and smiled. They all embraced each other and called it a night.

7

COMBAT MISSIONS

THEY WOKE UP VERY EARLY AND HURRIEDLY GEARED UP for Solon's ultimate day of preparation, as well as their last day of being together. Aristides performed several medically critical diagnostic tests on Solon. He even downloaded additional software for him. Aristides also double-checked that the installed device that prevented detecting unauthorized files was functioning properly, and it was. Moreover, Solon performed several other simulations in order to prepare himself for combat.

During lunch, Aphrodite bestowed a silver Saint Michael medallion to Solon that she expressed was blessed by a priest. Solon said nothing, and just embraced his mother and wore the medallion with devotion. Aphrodite reminded him that no one could ever know that he had a religious medallion. Like other draconian laws, it was a capital offense.

Aphrodite prayed to herself, *"God, please watch over our son with Your rod and staff. May he only fight for Your glory and will. Lord, please save him and please forgive his actions and save his soul.*

Solon persistently practiced for the next several hours. At 1900, Solon said his goodbyes to his parents. They prayed together by reciting the Our Father and Psalm 23 as they held hands.

AI Thirteen and Solon left for the muster at 2100. AI Thirteen would be authorized to be Solon's aide since he was an officer. Solon promised to his parents to protect him and keep him out of harm's way. Solon reported to the mustering officer, and they boarded a highly armed combat aircraft for the war zone, which was supposedly over six thousand miles away. The combat zone was called the PATRIOT ZONE. However, the soldiers called it the GRIM REAPER ZONE. In less than an hour, Solon arrived at the GRIM REAPER ZONE. As the aircraft was landing, it was hit by small arms fire but did not sustain any significant damage.

During the same evening, Lieutenant Colonel Moros and his deadly unit were performing one of the primary goals of the ELITE, hunting and terminating unauthorized humans. This depopulation unit, like a few others, did not fall under the generals and military command. This unit was under direct control of ELITE Seth. This unit had discovered another unauthorized human community that was deep in a thick jungle. These discovered humans were unvaccinated, had no biometric chips, and were not AE HUMANS. Moreover, these humans claimed no allegiance to any EMPIRE. There were extended families, children, and even the elderly. For the sixth time this year, he gave the lethal order to exterminate them all without remorse. As expected, the barbaric unit showed no mercy, except for one new conscientious soldier. Lieutenant Colonel immediately shot the merciful soldier. All the other soldiers heeded to the warning, which resulted in 372 deaths. The corpses were gathered for the satanic ELITES. These bodies were shipped to the ELITES for their satanic feasts.

At 2300 hours, Solon reported to his battalion commander. Lieutenant Colonel Apollo lectured, "Lieutenant, welcome to hell and the GRIM REAPER ZONE! I have reviewed your records, which are extremely impressive. However, I do not give a damn. It is meaningless to me.

"You are Lieutenant **316**. Lieutenant **316**, you will be referred by me and other battalion staff as Lieutenant **316** until you survive at least thirty days. You only have a twenty-five percent chance of enduring and surviving thirty days. If thirty days pass and you are fortunate enough to still be alive, I promise to call you by your name, and I will want to know who you are since you will be a brother in arms and a fellow warrior. Until then, you are just one more in the meat grinder and a soul for the grim reaper!

"I do not care who you are until then. I have lost too many soldiers and officers to care. After thirty days, you are human to me.

"One other reality for you: If you somehow survive thirty days, then you have a fifty-fifty chance of making it four years. However, I care and am motivated enough to perform my best for you to survive your enlistment time and be allowed to leave this dismal hell.

"You have been assigned to Captain Nike. This unit has a critical mission soon, like always, on which the captain will brief you. This mission supports our war against the Aztec Empire, which is why we are in the REAPER ZONE. Make sure that the mission is a success or it will be your last one! Understood?"

Solon replied, "Yes, sir!"

Lieutenant Colonel Apollo continued, "One additional piece of advice: Listen to seasoned sergeants. They will keep you alive. If you do something stupid or cowardly that adversely affects the unit, I will kill you myself. You are dismissed, and report to your captain."

Solon reported to Captain Nike. Captain Nike stated respectfully, "Lieutenant, welcome to the Company Alpha Omegas. I am extremely impressed with your service record. You are the highest decorated lieutenant with no combat experience that I have ever seen or known. I had the honor of watching your Gladiator Challenge, which was extremely impressive!

"The higher has expressed that I must certify that you obtain a plethora of combat experience. Furthermore, the higher and well-known Honorable ELITE Heraclitus wants and demands that you be in the Gladiator games again. You should be proud of that rare bronze gladiator badge, which is extremely impressive! By the way, I promise that their wishes shall be achieved.

"You will be assigned to my best platoon and work with my top platoon sergeant. Sergeant First Class Ares has over three years of combat experience and is highly decorated. His enlistment time is complete in March. Keep him alive at all costs; however, always put the mission first. Sergeant Ares deserves to be glorified for his outstanding and exceptional military service, or at least die with glory and honor.

"Great, Sergeant Ares, come in and meet your new lieutenant and platoon leader. Solon, I shall explain to you your first mission, which is extremely critical, as expected. Be aware that this critical mission is to destroy another Aztec Empire unit. Look at the holographic table, especially the highlighted red area. Your objective is to eliminate the enemy platoon located here on this ridge. You must establish that they are reduced to being combat ineffective or eliminated. Your platoon will move out by 1800 tomorrow. Solon, make sure that the entire platoon understands the mission, and they have all their combat gear, as well as that they are all well rested and prepared. Good luck and STATE-speed! HAIL TO THE GREAT STATE! You are both dismissed."

Sergeant Ares advised respectfully, "Lieutenant, sir, welcome to First Platoon. You are my tenth platoon leader. Captain Nike and two others are still alive and promoted.

"We are the First Platoon Devil Dogs. You have been a legend since your assigned platoon saw you in the Gladiator Challenge. Sir, I was extremely impressed with your tactics and warrior skills; however, sir, with all due respect, you need to understand that this is combat against well-trained enemy warriors. Your last killing, while unbelievably impressive, was truly cocky and showy. That stunt was truly entertaining for the ELITE and honored guests.

"In combat, we shall just kill and neutralize the enemy. Sir, I have no desire to risk the lives of this unit in order to be an eye-catching warrior scene.

"After saying that, you shall be a great platoon leader if you sincerely care and trust these exceptional combat veteran soldiers. These soldiers will kill and die for you. We are a cohesive unit and team."

Solon responded sincerely, "Thank you for your insight and experience. I promise to care for and trust the unit, and we shall safeguard that the mission is accomplished. We are a team!"

Sergeant responded, "Yes, sir! We shall prepare the unit and inform them of the upcoming mission. Sir, we have your back."

They met with First Platoon, which was well known as the infamous deadly Devil Dogs. They briefed them on the critical mission and started preparing for the mission. The next day, the platoon was well rested and well fed. Diligently, the platoon performed several maneuvers and platoon tactics to prepare for the critical mission. The platoon's teamwork was undeniably like a well-oiled machine. Several of the soldiers greeted Lieutenant Solon with a cautious demeanor.

The unit moved out by 1500 to their predetermined objective. They arrived at their objective by sunset and spearheaded with military precision into a superb defensive camouflaged position. The Devil Dog platoon was in visual range of the enemy platoon. The foe was not aware of their presence or existence.

Lieutenant Solon ordered the first squad to stealthily outflank the enemy platoon. The enemy was not in any defensive position, and the unsuspecting foe were eating their meals and relaxing with no security. Sergeant Ares purposely left with the first squad. Once the first squad was at a flanking location, Sergeant Ares ordered the first squad to open fire, which resulted in the rival platoon retreating toward the rest of the Devil Dog platoon. Once the enemy platoon was merely ten yards away, Lieutenant Solon ordered the Devil Dogs to open fire with deadly accuracy. The enemy platoon was terminated, and the mission was a complete success with no Devil Dog casualties. Only two Devil Dog AI soldiers were damaged; however, the damage was not significant. All the Devil Dog AI soldiers were still combat ready. Sergeant Ares and Lieutenant Solon secured the top-secret plans that they discovered and requisitioned. After completing the critical mission, the victorious Devil Dogs returned to their home base.

Captain Nike expressed, "Devil Dogs, welcome home! Your critical assigned mission was an overwhelming military victory and success! You brought great glory to the EMPIRE! Go enjoy your well-deserved chow and rest! Your next mission will be in seventy-two hours! Sergeant Ares and Lieutenant Solon, please see me in my quarters. I want to discuss how the mission went from your perspective."

Sergeant Ares spoke first and informed, "The unit performed exceptionally with no casualties. The lieutenant was a superior leader and officer. His performance was outstanding, especially for this being just his first mission. Honestly, we were fortunate that the enemy let their guard down and we, of course, the Devil Dogs, licked our chops and took advantage of this rare opportunity."

Captain Nike spoke. "Well, lieutenant, what do you think?"

Lieutenant Solon responded. "Sergeant Ares was the true hero. First Squad and Sergeant Ares outflanked the enemy, which led to the enemy running into our kill zone. The rest of the Devil Dogs terminated the enemy easily when they were in the developed kill zone."

Captain Nike concluded, "Obviously, it was clearly excellent leadership and superior teamwork. Go enjoy your well-deserved meal and rest. We shall review the next mission tomorrow night. You are both dismissed. HAIL THE GREAT STATE!"

As they were walking to the platoon location, Sergeant Ares declared, "Sir, you did exceptionally well. I trust your leadership and I know that you will strive to keep this unit alive and successful. You are now officially a Devil Dog." He presented to him a Devil Dog patch and a silver challenge coin. Sergeant expressed, "Sir, wear this unit patch with pride and honor!"

They arrived at the platoon headquarters. They started preparing for the next mission. The esprit de corps was outstanding, and the unit had a very high cohesiveness and warrior brotherhood. In addition, the lion's share of the platoon was accepting Solon as a leader and that he would care for them.

Solon pondered, *I thank the Lord for giving me my parents, who prepared me for my challenging and daunting military service. I am extremely fortunate to be assigned as the platoon leader of the Devil Dogs and to have Sergeant Ares. I truly believe that my chances of surviving my service time have skyrocketed.*

I pray my loving parents are doing well, and I look forward to seeing them again. Amen.

Back in the city of **Utopianapolis**, Aphrodite and Aristides were missing their beloved son. On a positive note, their love and devotion to each other had been renewed since Solon married them. When Aphrodite was blue and down, she lifted her spirits by recalling the good times that she had when Solon was home with them and when he was developing prior to the initial awakening. Aristides's focus had been on his profession and enhancing other future soldiers, as well as assisting others. He comforted and expressed his love toward her regularly.

A couple times a month, ELITE Heraclitus visited Aristides at his office for secret medical treatment. ELITE Heraclitus generally brought a present, usually food or wine, to Aristides. ELITE Heraclitus updated Aristides on how Solon was performing in his military service; obviously, all information about Solon was non-classified information. The regular visits were a mixed blessing. Aristides continued to be proud, as well as pleased to be informed; however, any delayed updates brought anxiety and uncertainty.

Back in the combat zone, the Devil Dogs continued to accomplish their assigned missions and had avoided fatalities. However, there were three serious combat injuries recently; fortunately, all three were expected back to duty in a couple of weeks. Furthermore, practically every week, there was at least one lethal mission.

After eight weeks in combat, Captain Nike was given a company-sized mission that needed to be executed within the next seventy-two hours. The mission was to decimate an enemy company that was approximately thirty kilometers away. The enemy company had one less platoon. Thus, they were under strength.

After seventy hours, Captain Nike's Company Alpha Omegas moved out on combat hovercrafts with air and missile support. The Devil Dogs were ordered to move to an objective two kilometers from the enemy. The Devil Dogs' mission was to remain in the rear as a reserve unit until called upon.

When the Company Alpha Omegas were approximately one kilometer out from the enemy company, Captain Nike ordered air support to drop its payloads. The initial bombing eliminated one enemy platoon and seriously affected the combat effectiveness of another one. However, the friendly intel was in error. The enemy had an additional platoon, not one less.

Captain Nike ordered the Devil Dogs to move out and attack the discovered extra enemy platoon. Captain Nike accepted Lieutenant Solon's request to move out on foot and agreed to soften the enemy platoon with an air attack. The accurate air shelling eliminated a squad of the enemy platoon. Lieutenant Solon requested another air bombing, which was clearly danger close. Captain Nike concurred and ordered the bombing, which eliminated another enemy squad and avoided harming the Devil Dogs. Next, with a three to one advantage, the Devil Dogs easily eliminated the rest of the enemy platoon.

The company commander, Captain Nike, unfortunately, was not as successful as the Devil Dogs. His unit had taken out one more enemy platoon with the sacrifice of Nike's second platoon. Currently, both sides each had two mission-capable platoons. Captain Nike, with the third platoon, was engaged against two enemy platoons. The Devil Dogs quickly maneuvered on foot to outflank the two enemy platoons. Lieutenant Solon ordered an air strike from the rear of the enemy, which the captain concurred. This bombing took out another enemy platoon. This gave a two-to-one advantage to the Company Alpha Omegas. The final enemy platoon was eliminated; however, Sergeant Ares was seriously injured. Lieutenant Solon carried the sergeant to his hovercraft, which eventually resulted in Sergeant Ares receiving his needed medical attention. Unfortunately, Captain Nike was killed in the last engagement.

During the next several weeks, Company Alpha Omegas were reconstituted, and Sergeant First Class Ares recovered and was given an artificial right arm. Company Alpha Omegas lost sixty-three soldiers, which were quickly replaced with other seasoned soldiers. Once Sergeant Ares returned, the morale and confidence improved significantly.

After twelve weeks in combat, Colonel Apollo, who had just been promoted recently as Brigade Commander, ordered Lieutenant Solon to the brigade headquarters. Solon reported and saluted his brigade commander.

Colonel Apollo offered First Lieutenant Solon a glass of vintage red wine, and he articulated, "Lieutenant Solon, welcome to being one of my warrior brothers. Thank you for saving Sergeant Ares, who is also my warrior brother. I am sorry for our loss of Captain Nike. He was an exceptional company commander and a devoted comrade.

"Solon, my brother, you are human to me now, and I promise to care for your military career and existence. As I have stated to numerous lieutenants, I want to know you after thirty days.

I realize it has been over twelve weeks; however, there is a good reason for that.

"I have reviewed your records again. You and your unit will be awarded your combat badge tomorrow, along with a campaign medal. However, I must do something first. Captain Hermes, come here! Captain Hermes, read and publish the orders! Lieutenant Solon, attention! Captain Hermes, read the two orders!"

Solon was promoted to captain and awarded the fourth highest medal of valor for saving Sergeant Ares's life and performing several other heroic acts. This medal was one level lower than the heroic medal that ELITE Heraclitus awarded him. Brigade Commanders were authorized to award the fourth highest medal of valor with no higher approval.

Colonel Apollo expressed, "Captain Solon and my brother in arms. Congratulations! This is extremely well deserved, and I am honored to have you as one of my superior company commanders.

"For your information, ELITE Heraclitus, who has been monitoring your excellent military service, has instructed me to guarantee that you are in the Gladiator Games. I gave him my word, which is always critical and scary when your promise is with an ELITE. I know you will be extremely successful in the games.

"Your valiant unit will stand down for the next six weeks for Rest- and-Recovery, as well as to prepare for the games. Moreover, your company needs to reconstitute significantly and is currently not combat ready.

"In addition, I have been in combat for over five years, and the enemy normally stands down since they want to prepare for the March Martius Festival like us, which holds the Gladiator Games and other sporting and combat events. Your company will receive other soldiers that will be in the games. My other battalions will secure your company area while your unit will rest and prepare for the games. Keep this between you and me. ELITE Heraclitus and ELITE Mars have designated several satellites and air support to safeguard that our area is protected. Solon, do you have any questions or wishes?"

Captain Solon requested, "I request to promote Sergeant First Class Ares to First Sergeant. In addition, what games do you want me to prepare for?"

Colonel Apollo responded, "I absolutely concur with promoting Sergeant Ares. We shall do it at the award ceremony tomorrow. Regarding preparation of the games, you are our fastest soldier, so you will do some or all of the track events. You will be in the gladiator fighting events, which are similar to your gladiator challenge. Tell me which throwing or lifting event you prefer, and I shall ensure that you are part of that event. I understand you may want time to think about which throwing or lifting event you wish to do."

Colonel Apollo and Captain Solon conversed for over a couple of hours. The conversation was very revealing for both of them. After a couple of glasses of wine and insightful discussions, Solon returned to his company headquarters.

The next day, the soldiers of the Company Alpha Omegas were awarded their individual combat badge and campaign medal. Furthermore, several soldiers were promoted, including now First Sergeant Ares. Captain Nike was promoted to Major, which was awarded posthumously. After the promotion and award ceremony, Company Alpha Omegas were served an exceptional dinner, and the postmortem, the heroic unit, raised a toast to Major Nike.

The dedicated and decorated unit returned to their preparation for the Gladiator Games.

Captain Solon pondered to himself, *Well, I have served over three months in a combat zone, alias Grim Reaper Zone. I have already seen an unbelievable amount of death and destruction. I would be insincere and be a liar if I stated that I do not relish in what I am experiencing and executing. I truly feel that this is my genuine calling and purpose.*

I clearly know that I am responsible for my unit and soldiers. My teleological argument for my true nature is to serve my soldiers with duty, honor, and genuine leadership. They deserve no less.

I believe that the advantage of the first classification soldiers and third classification officers is that combat and military service has a natural and given intrinsic purpose over the other classifications, even the ELITES. I now appreciate why Colonel Apollo extended his service time. I may decide to do the same.

However, I miss my loving parents. I hope that I will see them during the March Martius Festival. Fortunately, the festival is basically in the same location as the Gladiator Challenge.

At least I have been able to keep AI Thirteen safe. He has been working all this time at the company headquarters. I have been able to keep him out of combat so far.

Back in the city of **Utopianapolis**, Aristides had been receiving the latest updates from ELITE Heraclitus about Solon and unclassified war situations. They were incredibly proud that Solon had been promoted to captain, as well as that he would be in the upcoming Gladiator Games. In addition, ELITE Heraclitus invited Aristides to be an honored VIP to watch the games with him, and Aristides accepted.

Aristides pondered, *Knock on wood. Solon's current and outstanding accomplishments show that we have prepared him well for his bellicose and demanding life. Solon seems to have developed to have a stoic perspective. He is clearly mastering his uploaded martial skills and tactics. He has a spartan discipline and honor.*

I pray that we are all united again as a family and Solon does not lose his humanity and soul. His mother's love will prevent him from becoming a nihilistic or psychopathic person. I pray that he finds his purpose and becomes a truly responsible adult and respected God-fearing man.

At the City Hall of **Utopianapolis**, ELITE Seth entered ELITE Heraclitus's office. ELITE Seth articulated, "ELITE Heraclitus, good evening! May Satan bless you! I heard that you have been monitoring the recently promoted Captain Solon's military progress. Are you planning for him to be in the upcoming Gladiator Games like Lieutenant Colonel Moros?"

ELITE Heraclitus responded cautiously, "Yes, he is performing well in combat and he has the experience of the Gladiator Challenge, like Lieutenant Colonel Moros."

ELITE Seth replied sinisterly, "I concur. Your special interest in his military service is noble. HAIL TO THE GREAT STATE AND SATAN!"

ELITE Heraclitus pondered to himself, *I do not trust that satanic bastard or Lieutenant Colonel Moros. ELITE Seth has no appreciation of will to greatness nor any appreciation of virtues like the martial arts or the fine arts. He only serves*

Satan. He views all AE HUMANS, even those with greatness, as sacrificial cattle for their satanic rituals and for their next disgusting meal. Admittedly, I do not care for the common or average human or AE HUMAN either; however, I respect the ones with greatness and will to power. In addition, I agree with the ELITES' objective to transform all humans into a greater specie, which is currently AE HUMANS.

The devoted, foolish satanic worshipers do not realize that Satan and God are dead. This resulted from religion seeking absolute truth with science and rationality; thus, science and rationality disproved God. Furthermore, humanity, which clearly includes myself like Frederick Nietzsche, has no remorse for the death of Satan; however, humanities' tears and my tears flow like a raging mighty river for the death of God.

I loathe and detest the satanic ELITES! I find the believers of God as merely hopeless dreamers who cannot accept reality; however, the satanic worshipers are enemies to humanity and are mere nihilists and hedonists.

As read in Mark 3:25: "And if a house is divided against itself, that house cannot stand." These are wise and revealing words from the historic bible; however, the solution may be in the next verse. Mark 3:26 reads: "And if Satan rise up against himself, and be divided, he cannot stand, but hath an end."

We, the ELITES, are truly a divided house of Satanic ELITES versus Atheistic ELITES. Humanity must triumph over nihilism. Humanity must exist for aesthetic beauty and art, as well as greatness!

For the next six weeks, the Company Alpha Omegas prepared diligently for the games. The unit was fully reconstituted and at full strength after a few weeks, which gave all the soldiers nearly a month to concentrate on the Gladiator Games and other events. The other battalions, under Colonel Apollo's command, had limited combat action. Their conflicts were mostly minor skirmishes with limited casualties. Colonel Apollo's predictions about the enemy's actions were, from a practical perspective, accurate.

Back with Lieutenant Colonel Moros and his malevolent and effective unit, they discovered the largest unauthorized human community, with 567 humans of all ages. Of course, Lieutenant Colonel issued the same merciless order, even with the begging and crying from innocent children. His unit had over two thousand scalps for this year. His lethal unit was clearly leading in the death toll for the year against defenseless humans. The ELITES, especially ELITE Seth, were very proud and pleased with their accomplishments.

ELITE Seth awarded a Unit Commendation medal to all members of the unit, as well as heroic medals to the soldiers involved. Lieutenant Colonel Moros received the second highest medal for valor and population control.

ELITE Seth pondered to himself, *Lieutenant Colonel Moros always fulfills the satanic ELITE'S ultimate aim, the purge of all natural biological humans. He is our greatest warrior and satanic disciple!*

During the training time, the **Federal Republic Empire** was increasing the patriotic propaganda and devotion to the GREAT STATE. The STATE MEDIA was in full swing with commentary about the future success of the GREAT STATE in the games. This tautological propaganda had the clear purpose of keeping the people in fear and reminding them who had the power.

Ironically, most of the citizens of the **Federal Republic Empire** were looking forward to the annual **March Martius Festival,** since there were no other holidays nor STATE-approved entertainment. All citizens were expected to exist for only the GREAT STATE. At least the annual games gave the citizens an escape from the depressing and tortured existence.

8

MARCH MARTIUS FESTIVAL

THE ANNUAL GLOBAL FESTIVAL BEGAN WITH REPRESENTATIONS of all eight EMPIRES with their respective banners. Following each colorful representative EMPIRE'S banner, ELITES paraded their respective athletes and gladiators. The spectacular and extravagant parade was led by the czar ELITES with their GLUE banner. Honored guests, like the czars and ELITES, were recognized and introduced by a sycophant announcer. There were flamboyant entertainers that sang and danced patriotic songs. Furthermore, there was an impressive light show, which was followed by a remarkable firework celebration that had a patriotic and demonic music track. The spectacular and ostentatious event ended with a STATE promotional fireworks show that spelled out *GLUE SPONSORED.*

Undoubtedly, the propaganda media hailed the three ruling czars when they entered the colosseum and remarked extensively on how great they were. The three ruling czars were the Archon, Polemarch, and Basileus of the GLUE, and they were the corporate officers as well. They had the power and authority to select the other ELITES and approved the recommended vanguards by the ELITES.

The second day, the games began. The first competitive meets were the running events, which lasted two days. Solon took part in all six of the following running events, which were performed in this order:

1. **6,660-meter race**
2. **Sixty-six-meter race**
3. **Six-hundred-meter race**
4. **Six-kilometer race**
5. **Sixty-six-kilometer race**
6. **Six-by-six kilometers relay race**

Captain Solon's performance was exceptional. He took gold in three individual events: the six-hundred-meter race, the six-kilometer race, and the sixty-six-kilometer race. Lieutenant Colonel Moros came close to beating Solon in the six-hundred-meter race, which was determined by inches. Lieutenant Colonel Moros finished second. Captain Solon completely dominated the sixty-six-kilometer race, which he won by over a kilometer. In the other events, Captain Solon took second in both the 6,660-meter race and sixty-six-meter race. Lieutenant Colonel Moros took gold in both events. In the six-by-six kilometers relay race, the event resulted in the following empires finishing in this order:

1. **Federal Republic Empire**
2. **Marxist Mao Empire**
3. **Aztec Empire**

Captain Solon and Lieutenant Colonel Moros competed in the relay for the Federal Republic EMPIRE. In the exciting relay, Solon ran the last leg and confirmed the victory. He passed the Marxist Mao Empire runner just a couple of hundred meters from the finish line.

On the evening of the third day was the spectacular award ceremony. As each athlete received their medal, their empire's banner was raised behind them. Once all three medals for an event were awarded, then the GLUE corporate song was played.

Commentaries from the propaganda media discussed the highlights of the events and advertised the future events. ELITE Heraclitus and ELITE Mars jointly spoke highly of both Captain Solon and Lieutenant Colonel Moros, while ELITE Seth only discussed the accomplishments of Lieutenant Colonel Moros.

Aristides sat with both AI Thirteen and ELITE Heraclitus. Solon requested that AI Thirteen go back with Aristides. AI Thirteen was now a loyal servant to both Aphrodite and Aristides. Aristides pondered to himself, *We are so proud of Solon's success! He has earned four gold medals and two silver! Lieutenant Colonel Moros, too, is doing extremely well! They were both exceptional in the relay event!*

ELITE Heraclitus expressed, "Aristides, you are clearly an outstanding enhancer! Captain Solon is dominating the games! If he continues with this success, I shall award Solon with something extremely special!"

The next couple of days were the first round of the Gladiator Games. Each EMPIRE had designated two gladiators. Expectedly, the two gladiators from the Federal Republic EMPIRE were Captain Solon and Lieutenant Colonel Moros. The first round was a gladiator versus six AI robots, which were actually six political prisoners. The political prisoners were captured rebels against the ELITES. Each gladiator only fought on one of the two days, and each day represented all eight EMPIRES for the first round. The only way Captain Solon and Lieutenant Colonel Moros would compete, would be in the final gladiator match.

Lieutenant Colonel Moros easily defeated his six political prisoner enemies, which was extremely entertaining to the ELITE and citizens. The citizens were under the impression that they were AI robots. Captain Solon started his event in the center of the colosseum. The six enemy prisoners had him surrounded. They charged at Captain Solon, and he jumped over the circled prisoners. He immediately slayed two of them from behind. The other four formed a line several yards away. He shot two prisoners in the head, which left just two more to fight. The two prisoners each attempted to outflank him from each side. As they closed in on him, Captain Solon side-kicked the one on his left. He turned at the right moment as he swung his sword, which ultimately decapitated the prisoner on the right. The last prisoner staggered to stand up. Captain Solon punched the prisoner in the gut, and as the prisoner fell over, Captain Solon stabbed him in his neck. Captain Solon was clearly victorious in the first round. Captain Solon pondered, *These AI robots did not act or die like AI robots in combat. They seemed human. If that is the case, I may have done wrong again.*

After the first round, twelve gladiators advanced. Prisoners that defeated any of the four gladiators were supposedly released to their EMPIRE of origin. In the next round, which would occur in a couple of days, four gladiators would fight new prisoners, disguised as AI robots. Since four prisoner teams won in the previous round, the other eight gladiators would be in a one-on-one gladiator fight against each other.

The sixth and seventh days were the six throwing and lifting events:

1. 6-pound metal discus
2. Mallet throws
3. Spear throws

4. Axe throwing

5. 6.66 kilogram shot put

6. Weight lifting event

Each of the events had six athletes from each empire. Captain Solon participated in the spear throwing, which was like the ancient javelin throw. As Solon prepared to throw, he contemplated John 3:16. Solon's longest distance won with a 316-foot throw. Lieutenant Colonel Moros won the mallet throw, which was like the hammer throw. ELITE Heraclitus insisted that Captain Solon participate in the weight lifting event. Lieutenant Colonel Moros won the event by lifting 1,666 pounds. Solon took second because he was not able to do his last lift because of a conflict with the final spear throwing event.

After the medal ceremony on the seventh day, there was a homemade incendiary device near the locations of the ELITES and czars. There was a devastating explosion with carnage and human mayhem. The broadcasting immediately ceased and went to the announcers, and the broadcasters spewed STATE propaganda. At least six ELITES died, and one was a czar. However, this czar was not one of the ruling three. The broadcasting ended for approximately thirty minutes. When the broadcasting began again, the propaganda media's narrative was that there was an accident and everything was under control. The games continued as if all was well. In reality, security increased significantly since three satanic ELITES and three atheist ELITES died.

ELITE Heraclitus pondered, *Unfortunately, I lost a good friend. I doubt he was the target. I, fortunately, left to check on something with ELITE Seth just before the bombing.*

Obviously, the rebels are becoming bolder and more

courageous. The rebels are discovering weaknesses in our governmental system, such as our occasional blackout of our surveillance system. This ancient, unmaintained system is in desperate need of being overhauled. Our overwhelming bureaucracy responds too late or not at all.

At least the balance of power has been maintained; however, the satanic ELITES will strive to blame us.

The eighth day was the second round of Gladiator Games, which was the sweet sixteen round. Lieutenant Colonel Moros advanced easily by defeating six prisoners again. In the second round, Captain Solon was scheduled against his first gladiator, who represented the Aztec Empire. In the first round, both these gladiators easily defeated their respective six so-called AI robots with ease. In the colosseum, Captain Solon met Gladiator Captain Poseidon, who was an extremely well decorated officer and in his second year of the Martius Festival. Captain Poseidon ran in the relay and took the bronze.

The two gladiators met in the middle of the colosseum with no firearms. They bowed toward each other and preceded in a defensive martial art position. Captain Poseidon executed the first move by attempting to side kick his opponent. Solon blocked the kick and hammer stroked Poseidon on the head. Poseidon fell back and regained his balance quickly. Poseidon attempted to punch Solon; however, Solon easily blocked and knocked Poseidon down. While Poseidon was down, Solon had his sword at Poseidon's throat and demanded that he yield. Poseidon yielded the fight and victory to Captain Solon. The crowd yelled, "Merciful Solon!" The crowd went wild. Even crowds that were rooting for Captain Poseidon were now willing to cheer for Solon since he spared Poseidon's life, who was a favorite in the games.

At the end of the second round, there were eight gladiators that advanced. The quarterfinals would be in a few days. Solon was the only one left without prior Martius Festival experience, and he had the lowest rank. It was customary during the quarter-final round to avoid killing the opposition, given the gladiators' popularity.

The tenth day was the first round of the combat squad warrior games. Each EMPIRE had one squad of eleven soldiers. The squads were organized into two teams of five with one AE HUMAN squad leader. Each team had an AE HUMAN team leader and four AI soldiers. Thus, each squad had three AE HUMANS and eight AI soldiers. A squad from Company Alpha Omegas was representing the Federal Republic Empire. Captain Solon's choice was Staff Sergeant Heracles to lead the squad. The object of the combat squad warrior game was to get your banner on the other side at the enemy's headquarter location without getting killed or eliminating or yielding your AE HUMAN squad leader.

The first two rounds were relatively easy for Staff Sergeant Heracles's squad. In both rounds, his squad won by getting the banner on the other side. Furthermore, they won by only destroying a few of their AI soldiers with no lives lost.

It was now the third day of competitions and the day of the finals. The Federal Republic Empire squad was against the Russian Soviet Empire squad, and their squad leader was returning from last year's games. Staff Sergeant Heracles's squad stealthily advanced toward the enemy's headquarters. One of Heracles's teams out flanked an enemy team and ambushed them. While the enemy squad was regrouping, the banner advanced to striking distance. The enemy team leader advanced toward the banner; however, in a rare occurrence, Staff Sergeant Heracles's overwhelming advantage convinced the enemy squad leader to yield. Staff Sergeant Heracles's squad took the gold.

As both squads were leaving the colosseum, a loud, devastating explosion occurred. It was another attack on the ELITES by the rebels. This time the casualties were low, with only one satanic ELITE killed and several satanic vanguards injured or killed. However, two rebels were captured and were immediately executed. The broadcasting resumed again in about an hour with televising of the executions. The propaganda media did not mention, like last time, any ELITES dying.

ELITE Seth thought to himself, *I lost a satanic brother who, like me, desired the needed culling of human cattle and to feed on their flesh.*

This satanic ELITE death has resulted in an unbalanced situation with the atheists who now have a plus one advantage. The good news is that Lieutenant Colonel Moros is being considered as a vanguard. He just finished his military service commitment. Vanguard Hades could move up as an ELITE. This should be voted on in a couple of days to avoid too much unbalanced power.

On the twelfth day, the medals were awarded late for the combat squad warrior games. It was delayed because of the rebel activities, as well as additional captured rebel executions, which were televised in order to maintain fear in the populous. Increased security was ordered by the ELITES. Vanguards were at high alert with shoot to kill orders. Surveillance cameras could identify unauthorized personnel. Unfortunately, several innocent people were executed merely for being suspicious. What the ELITES did not realize was that the careless regard for life was clearly exponentially increasing support for the rebels.

This thirteenth day was the quarterfinals for the Gladiator Games. Captain Solon's match was a decisive victory. He injured the opposing gladiator and had an overwhelming advantage, which resulted in causing the opposing gladiator to yield. In another quarterfinal match, Lieutenant Colonel Moros showed no mercy and slayed the opposing gladiator when he could have had him capitulate. The semifinal matches would be in two days.

The fourteenth and fifteenth days were the following four shooting events:

1. **Rifle event**
2. **Archery event**
3. **Pistol event**
4. **Throwing stars event**

Each event had two athletes from each empire. Captain Solon won gold in the archery and pistol events. The pistol event was exciting because on Solon's last shot, he scored a bullseye to beat out Lieutenant Colonel Moros. Lieutenant Colonel took the other two events and Solon took the silver in each.

The sixteenth day started with patriotic marketing that emphasized the greatness of the ELITES' leadership and their dedication to their citizenry. Furthermore, the propaganda media televised futuristic planned utopian cities that were promised to be available to the people in the near future.

Aristides, who was sitting next to ELITE Heraclitus, thought to himself, ***Obviously, the dedicated and brave rebels***

see vulnerability! There is such a disconnect from the ELITES'
central planning and the reality of how their planning affects
the people. Even today, the televised, futuristic planned uto-
pian cities are empty. These failed cities were over-budgeted
due to green initiatives and the need to be surveillance pris-
ons. The renewable energy is still not reliable after generations
of trying and failing. The ELITES' falsehoods of the supposed
utopian success only led to more lies, and then eventually hell
on earth!

In addition, humans are developing too many health prob-
lems from the ELITES' war on fossil fuels, eating meat, and over-
population. This has resulted in the vast majority of the popula-
tion having too high of a carbohydrate diet. This resulted in an
epidemic of obesity and diabetes. In addition, the green energy
initiatives have resulted in energy poverty for all except the third
classification and higher classifications of people.

Of course, like too many central planners, rulers, and
ELITES of EMPIRES throughout history, their decrees and
decisions had a minimal impact on their ivory tower, lavish,
out-of-touch lives.

After the award ceremony, several ELITES were exiting the
colosseum when there was live fire from a rebel sniper. The rebel
assassin shot three ELITES and twelve vanguards before being
killed. The three ELITES and twelve vanguards were all satanic
disciples, who all died instantly. Furthermore, ELITE Hades, who
was just elevated to an ELITE, was injured; however, it was not
serious.

The seventeenth day, the games were delayed while security
and clean up occurred. The propaganda media covered for the

ELITE and focused on highlights of the games. Security van-guards were arresting anyone who seemed suspicious or lacked proper credentials. In addition, they implemented summary exe-cutions of anyone who was in the wrong place at the wrong time.

As things settled down, the announcer declared, "It is time for both semifinal gladiator matches!" The first match was Captain Solon against another Aztec soldier named Major Vulcan. This match resulted in Major Vulcan yielding, as Captain Solon had his sword pointed at his throat. Of course, Lieutenant Moros showed no mercy again when he clearly had the advantage.

Of course, there was another horrendous bombing and additional vanguards killed and injured. This time, the bold rebels were not caught. The courageous rebels were discovering cracks in the ELITES' security on a regular basis.

On the eighteenth day, the announcer of the games pro-claimed, "The moment that we all have been awaiting, the Gladiators' Ultimate Game. Both gladiators are from the great Federal Republic Empire, which adores the GLUE! The two-time champion Gladiator Lieutenant Colonel Moros against first-time Gladiator Captain Solon. Both gladiators are combat veterans with distinguished military service. Both have been issued the fol-lowing weapons and gear:

1. **Helmet**
2. **Shield**
3. **Sword**
4. **Knife**

"They do not have any body armor. If a gladiator has a lethal advantage, he may request that the opposing gladiator yield; how-ever, this is not required.

"We have to give Lieutenant Colonel Moros the advantage because of his experience and significantly longer service. Let the glorious match begin!"

Both gladiators met near the center of the colosseum. Colonel Moros avowed, "I promise to award you an honorable, quick, and merciful death. I take no prisoners! You are already dead to me, which will soon be actualized!"

Captain Solon took a defensive martial arts position. They stared at each other for nearly two minutes, which created an unbelievably tense atmosphere. Moros executed the first move. Moros swiftly swung his sword, which Solon quickly blocked with his shield. For the next several moves, they swung their swords at each other, with neither one obtaining an advantage. Moros approached Solon close enough to slice him. It was a minor injury; however, Moros drew blood first.

Moros attempted to side kick Solon. Solon counter-moved by punching Moros, which resulted in Moros collapsing vulnerably. Solon pointed his sword at Moros's throat and declared, "Yield, sir!"

Moros immediately threw sand toward Solon's face and responded, "Never!"

Moros recovered and got to his feet. He immediately swung his sword at Solon's head. Solon ducked and thrust his sword into Moros's chest. Moros stood in complete disbelief for a few seconds and staggered toward Solon. Then he collapsed dead. As crowds were cheering and screaming, the announcer proclaimed, "Gladiator Captain Solon is victorious! Your new GLUE champion and gladiator! What a splendid match! Lieutenant Colonel Moros died with glory and honor for his

EMPIRE and GLUE!"

ELITE Seth thought to himself, *We, the devoted satanic worshipers, have lost six followers! The atheist must be delighted in the power imbalance, especially my rival, ELITE Heraclitus!*

I shall have my revenge by harming ELITE Heraclitus by any means possible. He seems to have taken a special interest in enhancer Aristides and Captain Solon. I wonder why? I need to investigate this situation and find a vulnerability.

After the final gladiator game, the closing ceremonies occurred for the next two days. The ceremony was grandiose, to the point of being nauseous and pompous.

ELITE Heraclitus expressed, "Aristides, you should be delighted with your enhancements for Captain Solon! I shall meet him later to congratulate him." ELITE Seth overheard the conversation and smiled.

During the final ceremonies, Solon was awarded the silver gladiator badge and the second highest medal for valor, and another medal for being in the games. After the three weeks of the March Martius Festival, the soldiers returned to their units with the realization that their respective endless war would start on April Fools' Day.

In April, the war was in full swing again. For the next several months, Captain Solon was planning platoon-sized missions regularly. His courageous company had few casualties. First Sergeant Ares took a position at Division Headquarters, which meant he would be far from combat; however, his time was extended for two more years. First Sergeant Heracles, who won the combat squad warrior games, became the top sergeant. The company's morale and dedication were extremely high.

Back at **Utopianapolis**, ELITE Seth ordered several vanguards to spy on guardian enhancer Aristides. After six months of surveillance and investigation, a couple of vanguards informed ELITE Seth of their findings. They discovered that AI Aphrodite was an AE HUMAN and was from the Aztec EMPIRE. Furthermore, Enhancer Aristides was having an inappropriate relationship with her.

ELITE Seth smiled diabolically and declared, "Arrest them both for treason and other capital crimes! They will be given a fair and just STATE-run trial and then be executed!" ELITE Seth pondered, *I shall have my revenge! We, the satanic ELITES, have not regained a balance of power! ELITE Heraclitus has convinced the czars to fill the vacancies with atheists. Thirty-six ELITES or czars are atheists. We only have thirty! We are a house divided!*

During the arrest at the domicile, AI Thirteen was at the office monitoring the event. His internal prime objective kicked in, which included avoiding detection. AI Thirteen was secretly weaponized and capable of self-destruction if needed. Aphrodite and Aristides had programed AI Thirteen to follow certain commands if they were ever killed or arrested.

9.

THE NIGHTMARE ENDS

THERE WERE SIX ELITES SELECTED TO STAND AS JUDGES for the trial of THE STATE versus defendants guardian enhancer Aristides and alleged AI specialist Aphrodite. Since there were only six ELITES in each EMPIRE, others were recruited from GLUE or other EMPIRES, when needed. The initial selection included ELITE Heraclitus, ELITE Seth, and ELITE Mars; however, ELITE Heraclitus recused himself and another ELITE took his place. Since ELITE Heraclitus was the Basileus ELITE, he claimed that he had a ceremonial event to attend, which was scheduled for the same day. The presiding ELITE who conducted the trial was Czar Dolos.

Czar Dolos proclaimed and declared, "Aphrodite of the Aztec Empire, alias AI specialist Aphrodite, and guardian enhancer Aristides, you have both been charged with numerous capital crimes and treason. The plethora of charged capital crimes comprises, but is not limited to, inappropriate and unauthorized sexual AE HUMAN relationships, harboring the enemy, and treason. These and other crimes, when convicted, come with a well-deserved death penalty.

"Obviously, we want to protect perceived justice and award you the opportunity to defend yourself or establish augmented evidence that will convict you. Aphrodite and enhancer, you are each allowed to speak your last words prior to our just and swift verdict and conviction. You each are given six minutes to speak.

Aphrodite, imposter AI specialist Aphrodite, defend yourself or request mercy."

While Aphrodite spoke, Aristides said the Our Father to himself. *Our Father, which art in heaven, Hallowed be thy name. Thy kingdom come, Thy will be done on earth, as it is in heaven. Give us this day our daily bread. And forgive us our debts, as we forgive our debtors. And lead us not into temptation, but deliver us from evil: For thine is the kingdom, and the power, and the glory, forever. Amen.*

As revealed in Psalm 86: You, Lord, are forgiving and good, abounding in love to all who call to you.

Lord, please forgive us for our sins. Lord, please welcome us into your glory and into heaven. Amen.

Aphrodite spoke with passion and conviction. "I regret nothing! You may all go to hell, which the satanic ELITES call home! We have lost our humanity! We are not allowed to love, to express our passions or joys! Our lives have no beauty or purpose anymore! We are not allowed to create art, music, or anything of beauty! Females may not be genuine women or express their femininity or fall in love! Women are no longer allowed to be mothers or wives or have babies! Families and marriages are not allowed. No AE-HUMAN may be intimate or have sex with anyone except with a disgusting tyrannical ELITE or vanguard bastard! Our men are used and exploited for your endless war machine! Many of our men have no constructive or meaningful purpose!

"You strive to take Almighty God out of our lives! You strive to replace the worship of God with the disgusting worship of the cold, heartless, soulless STATE or Satan himself! Thank God that you shall fail in the end, because God always wins!

"I have more respect for the atheist ELITES because they just do not believe in God and may still have some compassion and appreciation for humans who excel. On the other hand, the Satanic ELITES ironically believe in God! They have turned their back on God and worship Satan, God's nemesis! Satanists are at war with God! They think the humans are mere cattle for their future meals or amusement for their devilish games. They sickeningly believe that Satan will rule the world!

"I am fortunate to have loved a good man! I would commit treason with him again and again! You have lost your humanity and soul! You do not know how to love, care, or have compassion for any other soul because you have no soul!"

Czar Dolos proclaimed, "Aphrodite, your unmoving speech established for us additional evidence to guarantee your well-deserved conviction and your execution. Guardian enhancer Aristides, it is now your turn to seal your fate."

Aristides chewed a poison pill that would contaminate his body and any other flesh that it came into contact with. Aristides prayed to himself, *As revealed in Luke 17:3–4: Take heed to yourselves: If thy brother trespass against thee, rebuke him; and if he repents, forgive him.*

Enhancer responded with clarity and thought. "Czars, ELITES, and Vanguards, I shall begin by first framing my argument prior to expressing any evidence or conclusion. We must first recognize that the flourishment of humans' existence and betterment are the moral ends. This is a categorical imperative, which is my framework and thesis. If this framework or thesis is not accepted per se, then the alternative framework would be the antithesis. The antithesis would be that we do not seek the flourishment of humans nor humans' betterment. Thus, it would be safe to say that the antithesis would only lead to power and nihilism.

"After accepting the thesis, we need to evaluate all angles and perspectives, which include both advantages and disadvantages. This is to ensure that our logical conclusion supports humanity as an end. Furthermore, we should avoid and not desire that merely a handful of ELITES, czars, and vanguards have the flourishment and betterment.

"Let us compare our current situation to approximately eighty years ago. The world had nearly eight billion people with no current AE HUMAN enhancements or any AE ELITES. You claim that the world is held at four billion people currently, which is half of the world's largest population ever. However, that is completely inaccurate because the current world population is around 666 million. In addition, there are not eight empires in the world. There are only four empires, which have been in an endless war to maintain the low world population and hunt down humans who have not been enhanced with biometric monitoring devices. If you truly believe in your system, why would you need to lie or be deceptive about it? In addition, you violated one of Sun Tzu's axioms by engaging in endless wars: *'There is no instance of a nation benefiting from prolonged warfare.'*

"In the past, humans had families, friends, relatives, and other human relationships. Today, these types of human relations and others have been deemed undesirable and illegal. Admittedly, each one of these relationship types had flaws, which is expected since humans are flawed. However, you have denied one of man's basic natures, which is to be a social animal. This has resulted in denying the benefits of being alive by having genuine human relationships. You have doomed everyone, including yourself, to a lonely existence. Moreover, this has doomed us to being paranoid and loveless.

"Furthermore, everyone is required to have biometrics and chips installed. You are able to monitor all vital activity in their economic activities. Moreover, many AE HUMANS are merely biological computers with no self-control or free will.

"This total experimental utopian failure is clearly the result of abandoning the truth, freedom, and responsibility in exchange for power for power's sake.

"Starting over eighty years ago, ELITES believed in and built an entire society and world on falsehoods and deceptions in order to fulfill the ELITES' agenda at any cost. ELITES had propaganda media and internet platforms spew lies and label anyone who disagreed as misinformation in order to prevent any truth contrary to your agenda. This safeguarded the ELITES' power and political agenda.

"For example, for the last several years, the brave, rebellious rebels have assassinated ELITES and vanguards; however, the media have covered it up and always expressed how wonderful our ELITES are and how outstanding everything is. Furthermore, any information that countered eating synthetic food or supporting eating meat has been deemed as misinformation or squelched.

"For over a hundred plus years, we have strived to be net zero, which has only left the populous in poverty, as well as energy deprived. In addition, deprivation of meat and increased synthetic foods has resulted in people being obese and other health problems.

"You claim that all your actions are from a utilitarian thought process. You advocate for the 'greatest happiness for the greatest number of people.' However, all of your actions work to ensure that you maintain your power and your will and desires at the sacrifice of the populous.

"For example, many capital crimes are only applicable for the AE HUMANS. AE HUMANS are executed for wearing the wrong colors or having intimate relationships with each other; however, ELITES are exempt. ELITES and vanguards are armed. The people have no right to bear arms or the freedom of speech or religion. The ELITES have established a plethora of draconian laws. This clearly violated Cicero's axiom and warning: *More laws, less justice.*'"

Aristides thought to himself, *I cannot express the words of Solon of Athens, since this may endanger my son, Solon. The ELITES' laws lived up to Solon of Athens' observation and warning: "Laws are like spiders' webs: If some poor weak creature comes up against them, it is caught; but a big one can break through and get away."*

Aristides continued, "Your grand experiment is a complete failure and disaster because you were devoted to iconoclasts and tyrannical elitists. This even violates Thomas Hobbes' social contract theory; even he believed in absolute power for the sovereign. Our current ELITE sovereigns do not protect their people and are willing to terminate them at will. At least Thomas Hobbes believed that a citizen could defend himself when the sovereign declared to terminate him or her.

"This is not a utopia; this is tantamount to hell. Matter of fact, a utopia on earth is merely a pipedream with an ideological delusion that is always best for the elite of the elite. The human race is not transforming into a better species. You are just destroying our humanity."

The ELITE judges cast their judgement with dead silence for only sixty-six seconds. Then Czar Dolos diabolically declared, "Before I render the lawful and just verdict, I shall ensure that you hear our truth and our reality. We, the ELITE, do not give a damn. Humans are for our purpose and are merely our cattle. We are the uber mensch! The human cattle shall be culled at our will. We possess the will to power. AE HUMANS are all nothing to us and merely parasites. We decide what our utopia will be, even if it means that humans are condemned to a hellish existence. We shall always carpe diem! Thus, our power shall protect your antithesis. We do not give a damn about human flourishment or betterment. Humans exist for our means to safeguard our ends. Since God is dead or meaningless to us, we have become your gods to serve and worship.

"**I shall paraphrase John Milton's famous quote from *Paradise Lost* to guarantee your understanding before your inevitable demise: We, the ELITES, better reign in hell on earth to ensure humanity's dystopia, than to serve in heaven on earth for a humanity's utopia.**

"Therefore, because of a six to zero decision, as expected, you both have been condemned to death. This sentence shall be executed immediately. May the state have mercy on your existence, not really!"

Aphrodite and Aristides experienced a blinding, brilliant light. They both experienced a gruesome electrocution, which resulted in their agonizing death through silent screams of pain. Their lifeless bodies were immediately lowered to the location where their corpses were prepared for that night's satanic feast. Their flesh and blood, with the remains of numerous others, were mixed and prepared for the evening's hideous ritual and satanic banquet.

Meanwhile, AI Thirteen was able to obtain the video log of the trial with the soundtrack. Like clockwork, AI Thirteen was following all the directives that Aristides established.

This devilish and gloomy evening, seventeen satanic ELITES gathered for the feast and ritual. Unfortunately, ELITE Seth was running late. When he arrived, he discovered that all seventeen elites had been poisoned to death. Furthermore, numerous satanic vanguards met the same fate. ELITE Seth screamed hellishly and revengefully, **"I swear to Satan! ELITE Heraclitus, you will pay dearly! You did this since you declined to be a judge! I shall have my revenge and devour your lifeless flesh and drink your delicious blood! The house has been divided too long! Death to all atheist ELITES!"**

The elites were clearly divided into two camps that were assassinating each other; the satanic civil war was the satanists versus atheists. Fortunately, before the potential civil war started, AI Thirteen was able to warn Captain Solon via email of the satanic ELITES' warring intents. Captain Solon now knew that he was an orphan. Captain Solon said a prayer for his parents and vowed that he would make this right by destroying the ELITE system that had a stranglehold on humanity. Fortunately for ELITE Heraclitus, he was monitoring ELITE Seth and heard his evil intentions. All the ELITES monitored and spied on each other since there was no trust, especially between atheists and satanists.

The Satanic War raged on! This new civil war was among the ELITES. While the ELITES were butchering each other, AI Thirteen broke through the security system. Based on Aristides' preprogrammed commands, AI Thirteen established that the trial had been broadcast to all the citizens worldwide repeatedly and continuously. After playing numerous times, there was a media blackout; however, the message and truth were heard.

At the PATRIOTIC ZONE, the military generals and colonels of both Federal Republic EMPIRE and Aztec EMPIRE met and had a ceasefire, since they had seen the trial and both sides now knew where their loyalty should be. That loyalty was with the human race. The commanding generals strived to contact the other two empires, which were the **Germanic Nazi EMPIRE** and **Raising Son Maoist EMPIRE**. They failed. However, there was evidence that there was a ceasefire in their war. The other four EMPIRES did not realistically exist and were only phony nations in order to deceive the people. These four phony nations were represented by clones to other human experiments at the games or resided at the GLUE's headquarters. These nations were used to test and experiment with potential AE HUMAN changes.

The generals on both sides discovered the truth. The ELITES wanted a utopia for themselves at the expense of freedom and causing the suffering of everyone else. As the generals were convening, the soldiers figured out how to deactivate the installed destruction devices. Unfortunately, the ELITES discovered that the generals were planning to overthrow the ELITES. They immediately activated the destruction devices and killed all the generals. This resulted in placing Colonel Apollo in charge.

In **Utopianapolis**, the people were rioting and protesting in the streets. The vanguards could not control the people since they were outnumbered thousands to one.

Back at Company Alpha Omega's headquarters, Captain Solon was conversing with a few of his trusted soldiers. They were discussing what they should do, since the citizens of their nation were being killed and exploited by the vanguards. They had all seen the video of the trial that united humanity. The soldiers wanted to remove the evil ELITES and bring back hope to humanity. Captain Solon expressed, "I understand your concerns; however, why fight an enemy when they are destroying themselves? Furthermore, remember Samurai Miyamoto Musashi's following two principles of the Dokkōdō: 'Accept everything just the way it is'; and 'Do not fear death.'" After forty-eight hours, Colonel Apollo came to see Captain Solon with promotion papers to major. After the somber promotion, they immediately went to business.

Colonel Apollo directed, "Major Solon, your unit is ordered to bring stability to the City of **Utopianapolis**. Be informed that the Aztec military shall do the same for their EMPIRE in the city named **La Ciudad de La Utopia**. We do not know the status of the two other empires; however, we believe that they may do the same. Furthermore, your dedicated unit will be authorized to eliminate any hostile vanguards or ELITES. Strive to minimize civilian casualties. You will also be given an extra platoon, air support, and hovercrafts. Moreover, both our armies have already destroyed the GLUE Capitol. We believe that all czars and ELITES of GLUE Capitol have been eliminated except possibly one or two. This joint effort was to prevent a nuclear exchange since the GLUE had all the world nukes and other world-ending weapons. Once you bring peace to the city, we shall strive to form a new reformed government. Since you are my friend and brother in arms, good luck! Humanity must be restored without tyranny and ELITES!"

Major Solon responded with a smile, "Sir, God willing, I shall."

Colonel Apollo smiled and responded with a firm handshake. "Godspeed!"

Company Alpha Omega changed their name to the **Company Liberators**. After eight hours, the unit moved out on four large cargo military aircraft that each held a platoon.

Back at **Utopianapolis**, there was total anarchy and mayhem. There was looting and rioting in the streets. It was a complete Hobbesian nightmare. The atheist ELITES were winning per se; however, it was clearly a Pyrrhic Victory. There were only thirteen or so ELITES still alive worldwide; however, the initial so-called worldwide 8,000 vanguards was a deception. Before the war, there were only 1,000 vanguards in each of the four world cities; thus, there were 4,000 in total.

After the war started, the vanguard casualties were mounting and the current estimate was three hundred in **Utopianapolis**. Furthermore, two-thirds of the vanguards were loyal to the atheist ELITES. However, the people were not taking sides. The citizens were attacking and fighting against all ELITES and vanguards.

ELITE Heraclitus was the leader of the atheist coalition, and ELITE Seth was the leader of the Satanic Coalition. However, the Satanic Coalition was truly a house divided. ELITE Hades was challenging ELITE Seth. Three vanguards that were loyal to Seth took the initiative and assassinated ELITE Hades. In addition, several of his loyal vanguards and another satanic ELITE were killed.

Major Solon and his unit were a couple of kilometers from **Utopianapolis**. Major Solon had a platoon to secure the water lines and power lines into the city. Furthermore, another unit secured the food storage plants and other utilities. Another two platoons secured the routes into the city. He requested that Colonel Apollo send company-size units to secure what the Company Liberators had under their military control. Apollo sent five company-size units to secure acquired utility assets, food storage plants, and routes.

After the companies fell in place, Major Solon's company went on the offense. While the Satanic Coalition was fighting, artillery rounds landed. These rounds destroyed half of their satanic vanguards. The Atheist Coalition took advantage of the situation by attacking them. The Atheists were victorious; however, they sustained significant losses. There was only Atheist ELITE Heraclitus and thirty-six vanguards alive.

Major Solon's unit surrounded the Atheist Coalition and, on a loudspeaker, Major Solon demanded their surrender. ELITE Heraclitus and his coalition yielded and surrendered to Major Solon. Major Solon thought to himself what he learned from Sun Tzu, ***The greatest victory is that which requires no battle***. Major Solon placed ELITE Heraclitus under arrest and expressed that he would be given a fair and just trial. ELITE Heraclitus requested that he be killed with honor and glory. Major Solon remained silent and did not respond to him. Major Solon proclaimed, "ELITE Heraclitus and vanguards, you are prisoners of war and shall be treated as such. My unit shall safeguard that you are treated with dignity, honor, and ensure that your basic needs are met. If you cooperate, then you shall be treated reasonably well as a prisoner of war. However, remember that we shall maintain rules of engagement and exercise self-defense."

A soldier had his back to a vanguard, and the vanguard pulled out a knife and attempted to kill him. Major Solon evaluated the situation and shot and killed the vanguard before he reached the vulnerable soldier. Major Solon stated, "That was a lawful killing! Take that as a warning!" After the incident, the prisoners cooperated, and they gave up all their weapons.

Major Solon's unit took over the media. Eloquently, Major Solon announced, "Citizens of the Federal Republic EMPIRE and the city of **Utopianapolis**, I have taken command of the Federal Republic EMPIRE and the city until a constitutional republic is established. During this transition, there will be martial law. The military shall strive to safeguard that the populous are fed and given proper care. However, we must maintain peace and order!

"Furthermore, we shall strive to inform you of the current state of the world. For example, there are only four EMPIRES in the world. The Federal Republic EMPIRE and Aztec EMPIRE have been liberated from the ELITES and the czars. The other two, Germanic Nazi EMPIRE and Raising Son Maoist EMPIRE, are believed to be in a ceasefire." He continued to inform the populous, to the best of his knowledge, what the state of the world was, even if the truth was hard to believe.

Colonel Apollo arrived and proclaimed, "Major Solon, congratulations! You have saved an empire! In addition, Captain Poseidon of the Aztec EMPIRE, who you were victorious against in the Gladiator Games, has succeeded as well! By the way, we still do not know about the other two EMPIRES, other than they are not at war with each other and they are aware of the videoed trial of your parents."

Major Solon replied with conviction, "Sir, I have not saved an empire, as this failed ELITE dystopian empire must die. Truthfully, this must be a **coup de grâce**. This ugly phoenix must never rise from the ashes of hell again. This ELITIST EMPIRE must never exist again! It must only be a historical example of what not to do; however, we must remember that we are all to blame and must fight the evil from within.

"We are just beginning the birth of a new nation that must be a constitutional republic for all its people with rights and justice. This nation must be built on truth, accepted proven principles, and wisdom of successful nations of the past. **Sir, we will, without a doubt, again be a successful great free nation. There is much work to do. Sir, we have just begun!**"

ACKNOWLEDGMENTS

I WOULD LIKE TO ACKNOWLEDGE our older son for inspiring me to write this dystopian book, as well as my family for their support and encouragement to be a stoic writer. Their encouragement and motivation even inspired me to found *Stoic Writing, LLC.* In addition, I would like to thank the exceptional staff of Columbus Publishing Lab, who were amazing in assisting me in creating this dystopian book.

ABOUT THE AUTHOR

IN 2017, the author of ***HUMANS' ENHANCEMENTS*** retired as a Lieutenant Colonel with over thirty years of military service. This soldier served as both a combat engineer and quartermaster officer. He is a combat veteran who was deployed or mobilized for nearly eight years in his military career. In 2004, he earned the ***Combat Action Badge*** and ***combat patch***. In 2007, he completed his highest military school, ***Command and General Staff College***. He is a Purdue Civil Engineer graduate, and in 1994, he was initiated as a Chi Epsilon, National Civil Engineering Honor Society. He has been a practicing engineer for over twenty-eight years. In 2002, he earned his professional engineer license. The author has additional degrees in Psychology and Philosophy from Valparaiso University, as well as a Master of Science in Management from Wesleyan University. In 2023, he founded ***Stoic Writings, LLC***. His beloved family is comprised of his lovely wife and their two Eagle Scout sons.

www.ingramcontent.com/pod-product-compliance
Lightning Source LLC
Chambersburg PA
CBHW020338260626
47156CB00004B/1579